UP TOP

CHARCOAL THE ELF

– a novel for all ages –

BOOK ONE: UP TOP

R. A. BELLSON

Single Helix Press

Single Helix LLC and Single Helix Press
865 West End Avenue Ste 10-D, New York, NY 10025
CharcoalTheElf@gmail.com

"Single Helix Press" and "Charcoal the Elf" and their respective logos are registered U.S. Trademarks

First printing, 2024
10 9 8 7 6 5 4 3 2 1

Visit CharcoalTheElf.com

Library of Congress Control Number: 2024913004
Bellson, R.A.
Charcoal the Elf – a tale for all ages
Book One: *Up Top*

ISBN 979-8-9910422-0-8 (cloth)
Single Helix LLC

Cover art by John Bates
Book design by R. A. Bellson

*To Peter Rezkalla and Dayle Vander Sande,
who were there at Charcoal's birth
and urged me on to tell his story.*

A NOTE TO THE READER

This adventure is the novelized version of Charcoal's actual narration, written with his assistance. It is intended to be read aloud to yourself or others when possible. Certain key words have been *emphasized* at our hero's request.

NB: Words included in the Glossary are indicated with an
*.

CONTENTS

AN INTRODUCTION
(literally)

"**I**'m an elf."

I was certain I'd heard him correctly. Yes. An elf.

There, in my comfy upholstered chair at the foot of my bed, barely visible in the darkness, silhouetted against the whiteness of my marble fireplace mantle, sat a figure. My intruder was smallish, about the size of a youngster of, say, thirteen or so. Why would a kid break into my home? Was he delusional? Was I in danger?

Softly and gently, he said, "I need your help. No, that's wrong. Not need, want. I *want* your help. Please."

It was an odd voice, high-pitched and hollow, sounding like someone talking through the cardboard roll left after paper towels were all used up. It was strangely hypnotic - it had a lulling effect on me.

"I'd like you to tell my story. It's an amazing story I think humans – I mean, people – need to know. I would tell it to you and you could put it into words that people will want to read."

"A story? What story? What are you talking about?" I said, running my shaking fingers through my hair trying to fight off the tranquilizing effect of his voice.

The final traces of sleep-haze had lifted from my brain. This was really happening. A stranger – a truly *strange* stranger – had broken into my home, entered my bedroom, sat in my favorite easy chair, woken me up, and was now commissioning me to write a story for him.

Gathering my wits, I forcefully pushed back the covers, and shot into a sitting position.

"I think you should leave," I said, as firmly as I could.

"Wait!" he said, a sincere pleading in his voice. "I apologize for upsetting you. It was thoughtless of me. I've traveled a very long distance and I was too impatient to wait until morning."

The hypnotic, soothing cadence in his voice was taking a stronger hold. Somehow my spirits began to lift despite everything and the remnants of my fear dissolved.

"May I turn on the lamp?" I asked.

"Of course," he said, "only, be prepared for what you're about to see."

Steeling myself, sucking in air, expecting the worst, I turned on the bedside light. Despite all my preparations, I gasped. A slender creature, humanoid, but definitely *not* human. Something *almost* human, with pointed ears, nose, and chin, light-blue skin and an amazingly thick mop of wavy black hair shot through with gray and white streaks was sitting in my easy chair. It was true. He was an elf.

"Would you like me to look human? I can if that'll help."

Before my amazed eyes, the creature blurred, melted, and rearranged itself, quickly becoming a young man, an unusually attractive one at that, dressed in blue tights, a cape with sparkling silvery flecks along its edges, and long, pointy-toed shoes, also blue with silvery flecks. Atop his head that same mass of thick multi-toned hair poked in every direction.

If I weren't so blissed out, I probably would have reacted differently. Instead, I simply watched, stupefied, passively accepting it as if it were an every-day occurrence.

The intruder smiled a ravishing smile that seemed to shoot right through me, lulling me further. I felt my body completely relax.

"You need some answers, don't you?" he asked. "I have something to show you."

He pulled a wrinkled sheet of discolored paper out of his cape and handed it to me. I could see faint blue lines printed on it, a jaggedy edge on its left side, torn from an old spiral notebook. A childish hand had scrawled a note in crayon. Dark orange. There was something very familiar about it …

It read:

Dear Santa,
Hello. I hope you are not too bizzy.
I know you are getting reddy for your big mishun next month.
It must be a lot of work too get reddy.
I would like some riting paper and some good pensils, please.
Also a sharpner.
I would like to be a riter when I grow up.
Your friend R. A. Bellson
PS I am five I will leav some cookis for you

My visitor continued. "I was in a storeroom yesterday and found this in an old file cabinet. A drawer opened and it flew right out and landed at my feet. As I moved about it followed me. I knew what it was telling me. So … here I am!"

I held the old, yellowed sheet and was transported back to the day I wrote this at the kitchen table, my mom helping me figure out what to say, my dad all set to trudge to the corner mailbox to post it. A tear welled up.

How could I refuse him?

And with that, dear reader, began the strangest collaboration I think anyone has ever experienced. Then again, maybe not so strange. As I was about to learn, elves are not as mythical as we humans think they are …

But – you'll find out for yourself. The **story begins.**

CHAPTER 1

BEING BORN

Elves can be *so* vicious! Whether they hail from the Sprights*, the Pixies*, the Faeries*, or the oldest clan of all, the Elphs*, one thing was certain: they were all convinced *their* clan was the best, and they were only too happy to state said fact as viciously (and loudly) as possible.

A case in point: Town Meetings. Free entertainment was a certainty at the Claustown Civic Center* whenever the clans gathered to discuss community issues. Insults, hurled across the Kringle Assembly Hall with its iconic red-and-white-spiral-painted columns and stalactite chandeliers, often took on epic, even legendary, proportions. "Your mother was an Ice Troll" or "Go jump off a glacier" are some of the more polite personal assaults heard at meetings. "You can expect nothing more from a Spright," encompassed a greater offense, as it skillfully degraded the recipient's clan while elevating the other. "Only the Pixies ever know what they're talking about" was the same thing from a different tangent. Heated arguments were often taken outside, where more than just insults were hurled. Piles of discarded snowballs often sat glazing up on the pavement in front of the CCC for days afterward.

The nastiness wasn't confined to town meetings or politics. Not at all. Elf viciousness permeated all aspects of the Claustown community. Something as simple as putting up a fence between two homes could develop into nose tweaking and ear pulling – despite the Non-Aggression Clause,* carved in ice many years ago to prevent just this sort of behavior. It had even been proposed – by no less a person than the namesake of Claustown himself – that the Claustown Bus Company create clan sections in their vehicles, or even schedule separate clan-dedicated buses, to address unpleasantness during rush hours. It seemed the four different clans were habitually at odds despite their common purpose and goals, which were, of course, getting Santa* (in his various incarnations) up and away at Yule*. Some believed it was genetic.

And so, the moment their new son arrived, Chuckles and Jolly Elph knew there'd be snarkiness to deal with. Always to be expected, but in this instance, they really feared the worst. Their new light-blue bundle of joy was different, and different was bad. As their firstborn, they couldn't compare him to any siblings, but they'd seen enough other infant elves to be aware he just acted so – well, so *different*. That was truly the word for it. He didn't chortle. He didn't giggle. He didn't play with his custom-made rattle (a gift from Aunt Delphi) or become attached to his reindeer "banky." He didn't laugh. Most oddly, he didn't cry either. He just sort of lay there in his bassinet and glared. Whoever heard of a newborn elf that glared? He glared at his parents. He glared at the nurse. He even glared at the stork that delivered him. His very first word, with Jolly and Chuckles hovering over him, candy cane and gift paper in hand to record it for posterity was, "Why?"

How's *that* for different?

He was different in another way, too. Although a healthy elf specimen – lean, lanky, with an especially attractive pointy nose and ears that tapered to the perfect pinnacle – he didn't resemble any of his cousins, which was definitely a red flag for gossip mongers. For instance, he lacked the rosy cheeks and sparkling eyes of Happy and Sunny's little twins, born last year. His cheeks were merely a duller shade of blue than the rest of him, and his gray eyes often glowed in a disturbing manner.

He didn't have the sparkling golden tresses of Eager and Busy's offspring. He certainly didn't sport the sparkly green curls of his "special" cousin Trixie – a distant cousin actually, on the Pixie side of the family – but why would he? That emerald hair of hers was so special Santa himself sat up and took note when she arrived down her parents' chimney. Yes – Trixie, although a new arrival herself, was destined for greatness. Everyone sensed that. No argument there.

But back to Jolly and Chuckles's bundle of joy. His cheeks didn't sparkle. His eyes didn't sparkle. His hair didn't sparkle. Nothing at all about this tyke could be described as sparkly. Just a soft blue – albeit a very attractive blue.

Speaking of hair … It was his hair, when it started sprouting a few days after his arrival, that was the real clincher. No one in the clan could ever recall, in all the years of recorded Elph Clan history (a *very* long time), an elfling born with, well, with thick black hair shot through with gray and white. It wasn't skunk-like, wasn't Cruella, and certainly wasn't zebra. Marbleized didn't describe it either. "Salt and pepper" was probably the closest term for it, but just barely. An infant elf with salt and pepper hair ... unheard of. Orange, pink, purple, magenta, blue – all common. Even the sparkling emerald curls of Distant Cousin Trixie, although unusual, didn't sound alarm bells. But salt and pepper? No. That was something totally and truly unique. And elves don't like unique. It challenges them too much. Too ... different.

Chuckles and Jolly were at a loss. It was bad enough being different already without having to be subjected to the scorn the other elf clans would certainly heap on their little son's singular hair. But what could they do about it? Hide that mop under a bonnet? Short-term solution at best. Elf children grow so rapidly. Besides, the bonnet itself would single him out for snide comments. No one used bonnets anymore – they'd gone out with hobby horses. Shave his head? Total baldness in an elf so young – that would be odd in itself, but worse, it would take a lot of work to keep that thick jungle of hair shorn. Plus, honestly, how long could they sustain that ruse? Futile.

Chuckles suggested coloring it. "A nice indigo, or maroon ... or even green like Distant Cousin Trixie," he said. But Jolly wouldn't hear of it. "I will not condemn my firstborn to a lifetime of hair dye just to deceive critical elf eyes. No child should have to pretend they're something they're not."

The immediate family fretted – and elves don't like fretting either – but despite all objections, Jolly was determined to accept her son exactly as he was, no matter how much he stood out from all the other newborns. She loved him all the more for his different-ness.

"Unique," she called him, smiling at her little treasure, who glared back at her. "We are all faced with challenges in life, and he will simply have to get used to being unique. I feel he has a great destiny ahead of him!" ("At least I *hope* so," she mumbled to herself.)

She even considered naming the tiny tot "Unique," but a name like "Unique Elph" wouldn't fly in Elfdom* in and of itself. Certainly not! Flummoxed, she was starting to panic about what name to present on Registration Day* when, luckily, her sister Glitter, while staring askance at the child one morning, mentioned in passing … "Something … something so familiar ... I just can't place it. All that black streaked with gray with white specks. I know I've seen it before. If only I could place it … Wait, I know! It looks like *charcoal*"

And that's how Charcoal D. Elph got his name. (His middle name honored Great Uncle Dour, who'd never had progeny of his own.)

CHAPTER 2

BEING REGISTERED

On Registration Day, all the new elflings were brought to Wenceslaus Hall* to be formally documented, introduced, and welcomed to Elfdom. By human standards there were just a few newborns. Elves are very long-lived and procreate based only upon need. It's a cyclical thing – natural selection at work. The North Pole*, with its limited space, could easily become overpopulated. And so, as I'm told, Elf families are small both by necessity and genetics. Their natural birth cycle, which causes all the young ones to be born just around high summer, suited the storks just fine. It would not be pleasant to deliver a baby elf – or a baby *anything* for that matter – in the dead of an Arctic* winter! And of course, there was Busy Season* to consider. The months approaching Yule took precedence over everything else – even newborns. Dealing with infant elves, with all their associated special requirements, needed to be over and done with in time for the production kick-up as Delivery Days* drew near. So, the annual half-dozen or so newborns were a welcome addition but didn't threaten the status quo. Except for one of them, that is.

Registration Day is always a day of great festivity in Claustown. Everyone comes out to see the small procession of little faces, meet the newest family members, learn their names, and, of course, GOSSIP.

"Ew – too bad about the Pixies' latest – did you see that nose? It's so round and perky. Not pointed at all!" Or, "That Faerie child – not nearly as attractive as her parents. Ah well, everyone can't be as fortunate as *we*!" Or, "What were the Sprights thinking, giving a name like 'Pretty' to a child with a face like hers?"

Ah yes … Elves can be – but, you already know.

This was exactly the sort of running criticism Chuckles and Jolly were dreading. They knew they couldn't hide Charcoal entirely, but they didn't want to make a spectacle of him, either, especially not on his coming-out day. And, to be frank, they didn't want that sort of criticism targeted at themselves, either. They knew that the Town Registrar, Chub E. Spright, would be bound to talk and Charcoal's unique hair would soon be the subject of wildfire scandal regardless. So, while the other proud new parents strolled to the hall behind perambulators, putting their newly arrived out there for all to see (and criticize), the Elphs, pretending to be "late," arrived by slaxi* (that's a sleigh-taxi for those of you who don't know). Luckily it was pulled by Comet, so they were little more than a blur as they sped through town. Still, the word was out.

"Poor Jolly – what MUST she be feeling with a child like that?" And, "I don't understand it. No one ELSE in that family ever had hair like that! Where could the child have gotten that mop, unless …" followed by a significant look. "And that *name* – of all the nerve! Whoever heard of an elf named Charcoal?!"

Ah yes … Elves can be – well, all right. I'll say it this time. Elves can be *so* vicious!

CHAPTER 3

TORMENTED

If you're reading this, the odds are you're a human being. As such, you might not be aware of how much more quickly elves mature than you. It generally takes only two years for an elfling to reach full elfhood. Of course, human beings take much longer. (Some, apparently, *never* mature, regardless of their age.)

Anyway, as the months passed, Charcoal grew right on schedule. Everyone could see just how apt a name he'd been given. Already sullen by nature, Charcoal's formative months didn't help. Not one bit. It couldn't have been much fun watching his fellow first-yearers giggling and leaping, dancing, running about, and playing with each other. Charcoal made a few half-hearted attempts to join in but was shunned repeatedly.

"We don't need any zebras on our team," said one spiteful Pixie. A Spright shot out, "Go play with your own kind, if there *are* any," and one of his own cousins said, "Take a long walk off a short ice floe."

And so, the lonely first-yearer found himself forced to

accept a solitary existence – and his potential friends were just fine with that. Apparently, he was fine with it, too. He discovered solitude could be very satisfying. He took long strolls on the pack ice in Claustown Park. He built an ice cave in his backyard and spent hours in it, just thinking, or playing with imaginary friends he'd build from snow.

He especially loved to contemplate the vista from his rooftop perch – much to the consternation of his parents (but what's to be done when your son is especially precocious at levitating?). The vast expanse of white sparkling as far as the eye could see, the shifting snow formations taking the shapes of fantastic creatures and castles, the beautiful glistening ice crystals dancing through the air with the breeze, the fluffy, cottony puffs of cloud emanating from the chimney tops all around him … they all seemed to soothe his soul somehow.

It's so beautiful out there, he thought, gazing at the distant stars twinkling above. *I wonder what it's like far beyond Claustown? Maybe there are other elves like me somewhere else?*

But his reveries were constantly interrupted by those insipid "ho ho ho songs" (as he called them) invading his space and distracting him from his musings. Jolly and Chuckles watched with concern as he retreated ever deeper into his own world. As they feared, he was teased mercilessly about his hair. Jolly told herself it would make him stronger, but it was painful to witness, nonetheless. And their sense of helplessness made things worse. There was so little they could do to help, except to love him unconditionally. They sensed a delicate, poetic nature in their son – "Jack Frost* painted the most beautiful pattern on my windowpane last night," he told his parents at breakfast one morning – which charmed them profoundly. They saw a gentle, sensitive soul and they despaired.

Out of necessity he quickly learned to hide his sweet essence. Assaulted by such negativity, as a first-yearer (a "Firsty" in Claustown slang) he didn't have the resources or experience to endure the constant stares, withering smirks, and verbal rebuffs from his fellow elflings as well as adults (who should have known better but clearly didn't). As we've definitely established, elves *can* be vicious!

Having never raised an elfling before, his parents were at a loss as to how to deal with this painful adjustment period. They would have even considered counseling if it were available to them, but since elf counseling didn't exist (no one ever seemed to need it before), they lacked that option. They had no choice but to be supportive and loving in their own, sincere way. They could only hope it would get Charcoal through what had clearly become a tough childhood.

Generally, he hid his hurt well, but every so often an innate anger would erupt from deep within. The first time another elfling grabbed his gum drops, Charcoal exploded with rage. He seized the thief by his purple hair, nearly yanking him right out of his clothes. Fists flew, epithets echoed, noses bled. The other young elves stood transfixed, staring with awe at this display of seething rage. When Charcoal walked away limping, scratched, scuffed, and bruised, clutching what remained of his treats, his perennial glare had vanished, replaced by a gleaming smile – the first anyone had ever seen him sport. He seemed almost maniacal.

"I won," he kept muttering to himself. "I won, I won, I *won!*"

This elf is dangerous, thought the other youngsters. *Keep away.*

Despite a stern talking-to from his parents, the die had been cast. The others knew Charcoal meant trouble. Wherever he appeared, a space always opened around him. When he left, an audible sigh followed him. He withdrew further and further into his interior world – not much of a stretch, since the others avoided him in every way they could - but he never cried, never pouted, never seemed hurt by it. Not outwardly, anyway. Chuckles and Jolly continued to fret. Deeply.

All through that first year, while the other elflings engaged in totally elf-like play, practicing hammering, sawing, painting, and singing – INCESSANT singing – Charcoal sulked. At his parents' prodding he tried, tentatively, to fit in, but the other elflings continued to shun him, now compounded by fear for their own personal safety.

Through that first summer he was constantly left out of elf games – no Snow Ball Wars, no Ice Hockey, no Polar Bear Plunges. Even the reindeer wouldn't let him join in any of their reindeer games. The other elflings began mockingly calling him "Coal-head" or "Anthra-sight," when they dared (and were far enough away). Charcoal merely held his head even higher, turned the gray flames in his eyes up a few degrees and assumed a challenging stance as a warning. It worked nearly every time, and he liked being feared. Or so he told himself.

With the start of school that autumn, things changed. He

was forced to temper his haughty defensiveness. The school principal made it very clear no acting out would be permitted – from anyone. Charcoal secretly hoped things might improve, that his classmates might get used to him – or at least get bored of picking on him. Maybe even accept him. His instructors clearly didn't. They learned to look slightly to the left or right, below or above when addressing him so as not to confront that shocking pile on top of his head, which only grew thicker, saltier, and pepperier as he matured. Charcoal could feel their discomfort. So could his schoolmates.

No open bullying was ever tolerated in the classrooms. Midday break, however, was another story. Now he had second-yearers ("Secondies") to deal with as well. Lunch and recess were a nightmare for the poor elfling. The only time anyone would sit next to him in the lunchroom was on a dare or as part of some club initiation. Flutter Faerie sat at his table one day and whispered, "Don't speak to me, don't even look at me. Pretend I'm not here. I have to sit next to you for a whole lunch period to get into the Elect Elves Ensemble glee club." Then she added, "Nothing personal." The day he sat all alone at a table piled so high with salt and pepper packets he couldn't see over them was rock bottom.

Why are they so mean to me? became a mantra for him. *I'm trying to be nice.*

He walked home alone after school every day even though several of his schoolmates lived along the way. At least he didn't have to take the school bus – that was a mercy.

Even his cousins avoided him for fear of what the others might say. All but Distant Cousin Trixie, that is. As everyone expected, Trixie Pixie was rapidly becoming the most popular elfling in her year — and it appeared, in all of Claustown. Everyone wanted to be friends with the little thunderbolt of charisma with the amazing, blazing emerald hair. In contrast to the abuse leveled on her cousin, everyone bent over backwards trying to outdo each other in fawning over Trixie.

She felt badly for her distant cousin — *Why are they so mean to him?* she asked herself often — and occasionally made it a point to sit with him at lunch or team up with him for relays or projects. She'd chatter about this class or that field trip, trying to get a rise out of him, and a few times even attempted a joke, her absolute favorite being "What's the difference between a human and a snow man? The snow man has a warm heart," to no avail. While Trixie nearly fell off her chair with laughter, her cousin raised nary an eyebrow in response.

As time passed, being Trixie, she became stubbornly determined to pull him out of his funk, even a little bit, and show him there was at least one elfling in Claustown who didn't shun him. It became a sort of mission for her. Being Trixie, no one *dared* criticize her. But no one dared follow her lead, either. In a way, her kindness made Charcoal all the more distant. He felt she was simply acting out of pity. Perhaps she was. He sank ever deeper into his solitude — a true loner. Unheard of in Claustown — but understandable. Who wouldn't react that same way?

For self-preservation, Charcoal assumed a cynical, aloof demeanor. For instance: While the others laughed and frolicked playing elf-games, Charcoal would stroll by and pointedly roll his eyes skyward — especially when the singing started in force. The elves had adopted a song by Johnny Marks from an old human TV special as their sort-of unofficial anthem. Charcoal would exaggeratedly plug his ears during the part about working hard all day but it feeling like play, and the endless "ho ho hos" reverberating around the Eager Elf Training Academy (that was the name of their school) were enough to drive him out of the room. And he made certain everyone noticed. *"Faren*!!!"* ("enough" in his native tongue) became a sort of unofficial trademark of his; he would exclaim it – markedly – so often.

* * *

Elfling schooling consists of two years of formal courses – the first being Introductory, the second Advanced Level, with no break between them. There's no need for elves to take vacations because, essentially, their entire existence strongly resembles one. When standard curriculum consists of subjects like "Fun and Games," "Balloon Inflation," "Merriment Enhancement," and "Stardust Distribution," a break between school years is pretty much a waste of time. Besides, where would they go? Geographically, their choices were quite limited.

As Charcoal and his classmates entered their second year, his chief instructor, Professor Sprite Lee Spright, noted a worrisome decline in interest and involvement on Charcoal's part. Whereas in first year he diligently completed all his assignments, striving clearly to outdo everyone else and take top honors, in second year he became rebellious. He returned his assignments half-completed or not at all. His behavior in class worsened each day. Sometimes he'd endlessly mumble *"Far-*

en!" or simply pretend to be asleep, snoring loudly enough to interrupt the instructor.

Once, in Sparkle and Glitter Application class, he faked a violent sneeze, blowing shiny bits of color all over the classroom. His acidic response, "Hmmm, I must be allergic to glitz," became part of the Charcoal legend years later. At the time the whole incident was simply obnoxious – and very messy. The rest of the class, even the instructor, sat in stunned silence, staring at the chaos of colors floating through the air and sticking to everything in the room, including themselves, not knowing what to do or what would come next. Charcoal, feeling very proud of himself, merely stood, sniffled, held a tissue to his nose, and majestically strode out of the classroom, not returning until everyone else, including Professor Twinkle (of the Faerie Clan), had cleaned up his handiwork.

His abilities and intelligence were without doubt. If anything, one could argue Charcoal was *too* intelligent – it all seemed to come so easily for him. He would hover in the background, carefully feigning ennui* but secretly studying the demonstration with deep concentration, and then, apparently effortlessly, replicate the project perfectly.

Tasks that kept his classmates knotted up like pretzels were equally painful for him because they were so simple. No one could saw a piece of wood straighter (when he deigned to actually participate), drive a nail more accurately, or paint a dolly's face more sweetly. He'd indifferently toss off a model train set or a dollhouse without a second thought while manifesting supreme boredom, and it would be the best one produced that day. The speed with which he completed his tasks, and the unquestionable quality of his work, were direct-ly opposed to the pleasure he seemed *not* to take from being so capable. He outdid the others simply to spite them. He found it all so trivial. *"Faren."*

And so, his report cards always sported A's in all his cur-ricular subjects, but when it came to "plays well with others," or "sings and dances with enthusiasm," or "manifests ideal elf-like cheerfulness," Professor Spright couldn't think of a letter low enough to reflect his begrudging surliness. *What comes after Z?* the professor caught himself thinking one day. Chuckles and Jolly – in fact, the entire Elph Clan – were deep-ly concerned and wondered if the tyke would ever find his niche in Elfdom.

CHAPTER 4

EXPLORATIONING

One lovely frigid and blowy Arctic day accented with hail, while on a survival hike with his schoolmates, Charcoal stumbled across the shattered remains of a shipwreck clearly centuries old. The other young elves nervously huddled far away in uncertainty – "Coal-head, this isn't on our task assignment sheet" – but he clambered about, fascinated by the smashed hull, split masts, and tattered sails sheathed in sparkling ice and being pelted with more. The shattered wreck glistened in the glittering late-autumn squall. The combination of sparkle and decay was almost over-whelming.

"The most beautiful thing I've ever seen," Charcoal called back to them. His classmates stared with open mouths – first at him and then at each other, knowingly etching little circles against their temples with a finger. How could he think this was beautiful when Claustown was filled with tinsel, glowing lights, shining glass decorations, and most importantly, candy?

Charcoal realized this was the escape from the commu-nal exuberance he outwardly found so abhorrent (although in which he wished fervently to be included). He needed distance from his unhappiness, so he took to wandering alone, beyond the confines of the Claustown walls, across the ice floes, risking the dangers of the wild North Pole to search for "the meaning of existence (if there *is* one)." At first the Claustown guards would risk their own necks to fetch and return him to the (perceived) safety inside the town walls, but they soon tired of his obstinate persistence and left him to wander alone for hours pretending not to know he was out there. "Maybe he won't come back," one of the guards once said aloud. The others pretended to be shocked, but in truth, it's what they all felt – and deep down, they knew it.

He wandered farther and further afield in search of wrecks, ruins, wind sculptures, and other evocative things that appealed to no one but him. He became adept at slipping past the guards at the main gates of Claustown, gaining expertise in invisibility in the process. Within weeks his sense of smell was so well-honed he could scent a polar bear half a mile away. His eyesight sharpened to the point where he could spot a pending avalanche or a menacing split in the pack ice far in the distance.

His telepathic skills improved steadily too, since he would touch base with his parents every so often (*Yes, I'm still alive*). His hearing grew so acute he could enjoy narwhals* singing to each other as they glided below the ocean's surface.

One day, they sang just for him:

There's one above, in search of love and friendship so deserving.

While we below, so much in the know, admire him unswerving.

Without a second thought, Charcoal responded, in their tongue:

You below, who claim to know, together swim the seas.

Here on the ice, life's not so nice, until I find more me's.

The narwhals whistled and clapped their flippers in approval. Charcoal was delighted with himself. "I'm a poet!" he cried aloud, flipping several cartwheels and taking to the air for a quick buzz around the opening in the ice. While he knew this didn't compare to the great poetry of the Elf Elders of Yore* (he had *devoured* the great sagas in Elfstory class), he'd never written a lyric before and thought it simply wonderful. *Even if I had to invent the word "me's" for the rhyme,* he thought with self-satisfaction. It was a good feeling.

As his explorations continued, he grew adept at snapping his fingers to make a spark and could start a campfire on the first try without a second thought. His igloos were always snug and cozy, using the super-heated edges of his hands to cut the solid ice into blocks and then finishing it by melting the pieces into a whole with his palms. His attempts at flying (the best means for reconnaissance) improved in leaps and bounds (pun intended). Without realizing it, his elf survival skills were being honed and refined.

He spent many hours contentedly exploring abandoned polar-expedition basecamps built by those pesky humans years before – their ruinous state, the beauty in their decay, and the non-elf essence of the camps fascinating him and lifting his spirits. One of the camps in particular drew him back repeatedly. It was sheltered by a large rocky outcropping, hence not as weather-blasted as others he'd seen. Although his instincts told him not to, his intense curiosity compelled him to enter at least one of the old, battered, half-barrel shaped structures. He didn't care much about the humans who once occupied this building, but he could see "stuff" inside through the frosted windows. The idea of a new adventure, which included treasure-hunting, was irresistible, despite the potential danger.

Entry was simple – the structure had been locked up tight when the last humans departed, but that was a very long time ago. Age and weather had made it creaky, with gaps and splits in the metal skin. It was pretty simple to gain entry. He merely rearranged his molecular structure – shape-shifting was another of the skills he'd been practicing – until he was narrow enough to slide through one of the gaping splits – carefully, as they had sharp edges. Once inside he proceeded cautiously. He knew he was taking a big risk and felt an urgent need to be on guard – watching for booby traps or hazards of some unfamiliar kind. Or creatures … polar bears *love* tasty young elves. Certainly, there was a probability the building was no longer stable. All his senses were on ultra-high alert.

If the camp appeared derelict from the exterior, it was possibly even worse inside. There was a palpable air of days gone by, combined with a sense that someone had just shut the door and left yesterday. It was eerie. Desks and chairs on wheels were scattered about. Fuzzy carpeting, stained, with grooves worn by years of those chairs rolling back and forth, gave off an odd scent. *Human,* he thought. A hanging paper calendar showed a date almost two decades old by his reckoning. Walls were discolored. He could see lighter patches where rectangular objects of various sizes and shapes had once been attached. There were baskets full of shredded paper, but other documents of all sorts littered the desk tops, the floors. Everywhere, old sheets of paper, printed images and characters on them, contributed to the sense of chaos and decay. He glanced at a few but they didn't hold his interest. They appeared to be forms and reports, written in what he knew instinctively was English. No pictures. *Boring,* he thought.

Suddenly, a gust of fresh air tickled his face. Instinctively, he took a defensive stance, then relaxed with a sigh – down the corridor the roof had collapsed a long time before, allowing the occasional breeze to course through the ruin. Beyond the opening, a mound of clean, bright snow blocked access to the rear. From what he could see, everything in back seemed equally decayed. He wasn't interested.

Charcoal could tell this had been a "working" building – there was no sign of beds or anything that would imply sleeping quarters. Looking past the snowdrifts, he could read a sign over a blocked doorway – "MESS" it read. He recognized it as an English word and wasn't sure exactly what it meant in this instance, although he thought, *What a perfect sign to hang here. This certainly* is *a mess!* Just the same, Charcoal made a mental point to look it up when he had the chance.

What intrigued him most, however, were certain ivory-colored plastic rectangular objects on some of the desktops. There were buttons and slots and switches in various places on the objects, and each had a dark, glassy rectangular area on top.

Computers! he thought, with an exclamation point he could

feel.

Charcoal knew what computers were – he'd seen one at the Claustown Security Station, although it was much more streamlined than these. With things rarely amiss in town (apart from his own antics), the town guards were infrequently called to duty, so they spent a great deal of time in front of the computer there. Charcoal didn't know why, but they seemed to enjoy it tremendously, laughing heartily, totally focused on whatever it was they were doing, while the computer made all sorts of dings and rings and whistles and toots, playing adorable tunes (Charcoal thought they were *awful*). Every so often a fanfare would sound, one of the guards would cheer, shake his arms, and strut about a bit before they'd start in to doing it all over again. *Now perhaps I can find out what all that was about,* he thought.

It didn't take long to figure out how to power the thing up, and there *was* power – the solar cells mounted high above the building were still functioning. But there were no bells or whistles or toots. Rather, some whirring sounds, a sort of pitched tone, a few flashes on the glass rectangle and then some words materialized: "Hello Captain Petersen." Then an image appeared – a gray background with wavy lines, the word "Linux" lightly written across the background and a lot of small, colorful boxes with different pictures or letters inside them. One caught his eye instantly: "Mozilla Firefox."

He wasn't quite sure what that meant, but it was enticingly colorful and sounded like something he had heard the Claustown Security Force say. He knew they frequently used a thing connected by a wire to the computer and there was one attached to this computer so he picked it up — it was rather thrilling to handle something he knew had been held frequently in the palm of a human being. He felt almost dizzy — the sense of a different time and place, an entirely different reality, a room abuzz with various Captain Petersens, all busy and productive — threw him a tad off balance. The lair of a different species, especially one he'd been trained to avoid since infancy — the most dangerous species of all. Interaction with humans was strictly forbidden, one of the cardinal rules that even *he* understood was not to be broken. He tried to imagine what must have gone on in this space. He doubted all these Captain Petersens stood around laughing at the glass rectangle and whatever appeared on it. He could tell from those papers scattered about that most likely things here had been very serious and work-focused — probably pretty quiet. Boring.

Without realizing, while in thought, he'd been unconsciously moving the thing with the cord. Suddenly a new image appeared. It said "Sign In" and there was a line under it that said "User" with the word "Petersen087-39" already written and "Click to Enter." His two hearts were thumping. He didn't know how to click and wondered what might happen if he did do a click thing. He didn't even know what "click" meant!

He started twitching his fingers nervously in succession — one after the other. Wiggling his fingers was something he always did when trying to figure something out. Suddenly the thing with the cord compressed a bit. And it made a soft noise - *click*! Ah HAH.

Another window appeared. "Enter Password" it said, but the line where apparently one was supposed to enter a password had a row of little x's filling it – "xxxxxxxxxxx." Once again, he was stumped.

He started thinking and the finger wiggling resumed. Once again the thing with the cord clicked. The glass rectangle changed a third time and he was staring at a brave new world. He gaped at the image, thunderstruck. He began moving and clicking the thing with the cord. *What if I do this? What if I do that?*

At first, he explored slowly and with caution, but within a short time he was moving and clicking like a maniac – in fact, just like the Claustown Security Force, and he was laughing almost as hard, but out of sheer amazement, rather than silliness. He knew he'd be spending a lot of time in the future sitting in front of this computer. He shot a telepathic thought to his parents letting them know he was fine and would be getting back later than usual that night. Humans had become his new obsession.

CHAPTER 5

TREASURE

The weeks flew and Charcoal spent every minute he could spare – and there were a lot of them, since he had now started cutting classes – seated before that contraption, absorbing anything and everything he "landed" upon. He had learned about the "World Wide Web" – aka "the Internet." He learned he was "surfing," that there were right clicks and left clicks and something called email, very popular with humans, although he could imagine no need for it. It seemed cumbersome to type (he'd learned that word, too) a sentence when one could more easily just send it as a thought. It seemed to him humans liked to make things more complicated than necessary.

He also learned the thing with the cord was called a "mouse" although he couldn't quite figure out why. It *was* sort of mouse-sized but lacked a cute face and a red and white fluffy cap on its head like the ones in Claustown – didn't have a head at all for that matter – and with no mouth it apparently didn't need cheese or candy to function. Charcoal had tried.

As time passed, he found he was hooked – spending way too much time in front of that glass rectangle (called a "screen" or "monitor," btw). He was getting dark circles under his eyes, which didn't complement his light-blue complexion (getting lighter by the day from lack of sun) at all. His hands were starting to shake a bit, his vision was getting blurry, and a bit of a bulge was developing around his middle.

He had the good sense to realize he needed to cut back and get outdoors again. Besides, he had absolutely absorbed *tons* of info about "Down Below*" (as the rest of the planet was called), little of which made sense but all of it fascinating. So much in fact that he imagined he might even be in the running someday for "Expert Elf" regarding humans.

Time to go out and get some fresh air and exercise, he thought.

Hard as it was to tear himself away from the screen, he did – one of Charcoal's better traits was being extremely disciplined (in his way). Meanwhile, his parents continued to fret and hope that, whatever it was he was doing that kept him out of the house for such long periods of time, was good for him. They thought it best not to ask, as that would reinforce trust between them – and they truly *did* trust their son.

"If I ever saw a young elf who could fend for himself, it's our son!" exclaimed Chuckles.

Charcoal seemed in better spirits, definitely – although looking a bit run-down. Ultimately, he worked out a schedule, splitting his time between his "research" with long breaks to continue exploring his natural environment. He noted there was plenty of misinformation about that subject "online." Specifically, there was a complete lack of information about Claustown on the web. It didn't appear on any maps, and it never turned up when he did searches, not even as a footnote (except as the surname of an ancient family in the Orkneys – whatever that was). Incredibly, it seemed the whole idea of Santa's hometown was considered fictional among humans, merely a subject for "fairy" tales – many couldn't even spell "faerie" correctly!

It was on one of his "explorations," as he called them, that Charcoal found the treasure. No other elf would have bothered to bend over to look more closely but there, at Charcoal's feet – actually buried under a few inches of ice – something dark and rectangular called to him. Through the frozen water he couldn't tell quite what it was, but it resembled a beat-up old box or casket blackened with age. It was irresistible. He *had* to see it, had to touch it, had to find out what it was. It looked so time-worn, so drab, so non-elf – in short, so appealing.

Recalling his De-Icing Class, he rubbed his hands together vigorously until they glowed, generating enough heat to melt the ice and dig the object out. You may not know that elves have a much higher body temperature than most every other biped* but even so, Charcoal was better at this than any of his other classmates – naturally. "Hmm," he said out loud to no one, since no one else was there, "Finally one of those dopey classes is paying off."

Once freed from its icy tomb, he saw the thing wasn't a box at all. Not a treasure in the traditional sense of the word, but he was extremely excited nonetheless. What Charcoal had discovered was an old book. Not any old book. Nope – this wasn't like *any* of the storybooks in the Saint Nicholas Memorial Free Library* back in Claustown.

First of all, it was much fatter than any book he'd ever seen before. It was thick with hundreds of pages – and no pictures. He'd never seen a book without rainbow-hued images in it before. The cover, made of cracked brown leather, had no brightly colored candy canes or faerie princesses, no quaint snow-covered workshops (which didn't resemble the real ones at all), no drawings of shiny new toys. No, this wasn't like any book he'd seen before. With a cranial flash, Charcoal realized what made it so different. It was a *human* book.

Charcoal had never seen a real human book before. He knew what they looked like because he'd seen them often enough when surfing the Internet, but the only books he'd ever actually touched or read up to then were produced in Santa's workshops to be sent to the domains Down Below where humans dwelt. Those cheery, colorful, silly holiday books held no appeal for him at all whereas this water-logged volume screamed for his attention. Maybe it had been dropped by an Arctic explorer or washed into the sea – perhaps from some wonderful marine disaster long ago, making it all the more enticing.

Charcoal was delighted. He was so pleased he danced a little jig around the hole he'd dug and promptly slipped on the wet ice. *Thud!* Down he went. Happily, no one saw his tumble (except that sea bird who was now laughing loudly). He tucked the treasure into his unicorn* wool overcoat where it could warm up and dry. He turned merrily toward home, and the prospect of examining his find under the covers by elf-light after bedtime kept him going right through dinner and homework. In fact, he was in such a good mood (for him) he completed all his assignments diligently and extra quickly and didn't add even one single mistake to irk his teachers.

Assignments completed, he put his candy cane down, glanced slyly at his folks, who were laughing heartily at a ridiculous human holiday special bearing no resemblance to reality that was being broadcast on Channel Yule that night, stretched his arms and said, "Ummm … I'm a bit tuckered out tonight, Mar and Par. I think I'll hit the sheets early." Jolly and Chuckles looked at each other and then at him. Charcoal *had* been very active the past few weeks, but tonight he seemed a bit odd rather than tired. All evening his eyes were positively on fire and he had rushed through supper and his homework like a snow devil.

"G'night son," they said in unison, Chuckles adding, "Would you like a bedtime story?" But Charcoal wasn't there – he was already upstairs in his room, the door closed and his jammies on.

"Well, I guess he's *really* tired," said Jolly. "I hope he's not ill."

Rising from the couch, she put her finger aside her nose and added, "I think I'll make some peanut brittle for tomorrow's breakfast." Looking slyly at Chuckles, she continued, "Assuming I can get some help."

"Can I lick the bowl?" he asked.

"Deal!" was the merry response, and out came the ingredients and utensils.

Meanwhile, upstairs … Charcoal was brushed and cleaned and jammied and ready for bed, the book nearly dry, although it smelled of brine. The pages unstuck themselves as he began to examine his new treasure. The first page had a sort of writing on it in an alphabet Charcoal had never seen before. It looked like this:

Отрывки из великой русской литературы

Now, everyone knows that elves are born with skills humans would consider magical. A very young elf thinks nothing of levitating or even flying for short jaunts about Claustown. All elves can converse with each other by thought – telepathy* – which comes in very handy when humans or polar bears are nearby. With practice, they can make themselves invisible and can even change shape – although these last skills are more difficult. Shape-shifting can be quite fatiguing, although some elves become very proficient at it and can hold a shape for a long time, even days, with a lot of repetition (though very few of them ever bother, because what does an elf need to shift their shape for anyway except as a party stunt or such).

As you can imagine, it also takes a great deal of energy and practice to completely dematerialize. Some elves never totally perfect it – which explains those unfortunate photos taken by two darling young girls in Cottingley*, West Yorkshire, about a hundred years ago showing themselves posing with fairies. That was quite the scandal in Claustown, as the rules are very clear about *not* revealing oneself to humans. Too dangerous. It took a lot of effort to persuade (you might say "brainwash") the humans involved that the photos were faked – because they weren't. It was a public-relations nightmare and many people to this day are still only half-convinced they're not genuine – because they *are*. Since those images were published, *extreme caution* is required when making Yuletide deliveries in Cottingley – that's for sure!

Anyway – back to the point – one of the things humans don't commonly know about elves is that they are fluent in every single language there is, and many that no longer are, both human and other. Charcoal, being extremely clever, had no trouble at all reading this unfamiliar script. He crossed his eyes, tapped his nose twice and read *Ahtryvski iz vielikoy russkoy literatury*. And being an elf, he knew immediately the book's title was *Selections from the Great Russian Literature* (or the Elvish equivalent). Charcoal wasn't entirely certain what this meant, however. He understood all the words separately but when he put them together, they didn't quite add up.

For instance, Charcoal could sort of imagine, for example, how a "Great Russian" could be "Selected," but he thought it rather rude that anyone's personal correspondence (*isn't that what "literature" means?*), no matter how great they were, should be made public. "Do these people know their letters are in a book for anyone to read?" he wondered aloud.

Puzzled, and tempting as this tome might be, he was now indeed fighting off sleep, worn out by a very exciting day. Begrudgingly, he slid the book under his tinsel-stuffed mattress to be examined further tomorrow evening. The Web was all but forgotten for the time being. He slept like a polar bear, nestled all snug in his bed, while visions of troikas* and matryoshkas* danced in his head.

CHAPTER 6

END OF SESSIONS

The next day was a busy one for the two-year-old elves. It was End of Sessions. School was over and they were to be evaluated for placement as apprentices to teams in Santa's workshops. There were demonstrations, quizzes, written exams, and competitions scheduled throughout the day. Specially invited assessors would appraise the work of the young elves. Donner and Blitzen, two of Santa's crack reindeer team, were to officiate as extra-special guest judges. Charcoal knew he should have begun studying long ago, practicing all he'd learned over the past two years. Just like everyone else he wanted to be placed with the best possible team – or, in his case, "the least worst team." But he hadn't been practicing. He'd been sulking, creating havoc, and best of all, explorationing. And, truth be told, he didn't really care. He couldn't imagine *any* team he might find bearable. It was all just so … so … *happy!* At this thought a little shudder ran through his body from his pointed shoes straight up to the peak of his unique hair. He already knew he wouldn't fit in no matter what his assignment. Besides, he didn't *want* to fit in. Not any longer. He was all through with that. All he really wanted now was to get back home and under his sheets and start reading that mysterious book he'd found yesterday.

First, though, he had to get through End of Sessions. That was a definite. He loved his parents, and he couldn't – wouldn't – do anything intentionally to upset or embarrass them. Cutting the finals would do just that, plus set the town's tongues flapping in force. He refused to even consider hurting them so cruelly. So, he went through the motions and participated in all the events he'd been scheduled for. He might participate half-heartedly, but he would participate.

Being Charcoal, of course, he rose to the occasion despite himself. He built the best rocking horse quicker than anyone else. And being Charcoal, his, of course, was one of a kind. He used black and white yarn to make it a rocking zebra instead of a horse. His fellow classmates were not pleased.

"No one told us to be CREATIVE!" one of them snapped.

"Some elves don't *need* to be told," Charcoal snapped back.

During the House Outdoors Decorating competition, once again Charcoal beat the others and with time to spare. Being Charcoal, he combined mirrors, prisms, and icicles in a totally innovative way, creating a display that sparkled and shimmered like the aurora borealis*. No one had ever seen the like before. His assessors crowed, the crowds oohed and aahed (despite themselves), and the other young elves lurked about sullenly.

"Anthra-sight beat us *again*," grumbled his cousin Glowy (one of the twins) to Professor Spright, "and he doesn't even *like* this stuff."

To which the professor replied, "Bear in mind, speed, quality, and originality are all factors, but elfish* *perkiness* is the single-most important consideration. After all, as they say, 'Jollity is golden.'"

Charcoal overheard this thinly veiled jab (as intended), but he just shrugged. *Faren!* he thought, not even bothering to say it aloud. Truly, he'd stopped caring long ago. Or at least, that's what he told himself.

As the stressful day finally drew to an end, the Wooden Soldiers Special Squadron (the "Double U Triple S") appeared at the golden main gates to Santaschloss* (as The Iceberg* castle was nicknamed) and blew a fanfare loud enough to crack a glacier.

"Hear ye, hear ye," bellowed the captain of the guard. "Tomorrow evening is the Great Selection Ball* at which all our elves will be assigned their new teams. I am proud to announce the Queen of the Ball has been chosen, (drumroll) ... and she is ... (fanfare) ... the one and only ... (sharp inhale by the crowd) ... Trixie Pixie, who will be the first-ever Green Queen!"

Although everyone pretended to gasp and there was plenty of sincere cheering, no one was truly surprised. Trixie acted as if she had never dreamed she stood a chance of coming even remotely close to achieving this undeservedly supreme honor. To be named Queen of the Great Selection Ball – and the first-ever Green Queen, to boot! Her smile lit up the castle gates and her clan glowed with pride. It meant she would light the star atop the Great Tree in the center of Yuletide Square*, she would lead the ball's entrance march, she would announce all the new elves' placements, and her own partner for the evening would bask in reflected glory.

She whirled and twirled and cartwheeled (thank goodness she was wearing tights), squealed and cried and boo-hooed like a giddy schoolgirl. Which made sense, actually, because she *was* a schoolgirl, although Charcoal didn't find her particularly giddy. In fact, she was the most level-headed young elf he knew and his favorite cousin (the fact that she was the only cousin who was at all nice to him certainly contributed). And though her display of giddiness didn't fool him, he actually smiled (well, almost) and was pleased for her.

When Trixie landed in a split right in front of him, Charcoal, glancing nervously around, helped her back to her feet. She was panting from exertion. Giving him a big hug (which caused him further distress and added fuel to the gossip fire) and her most ravishing smile, she batted her big green eyes, looked deeply into his own gray ones and said, "Cousin, whom are you going to the ball with?"

All he could muster as a reply was, "Huh?"

"The ball!" she said. "The Great Selection Ball. Whom have you asked to the ball?"

She fluttered her eyes again, cocked her head sideways, ensuring that her sparkling green hair bounced fetchingly hither and yon and waited for the expected response. She truly liked Charcoal – it was probably his intelligence, but his aloofness and surliness added to his appeal – a "bad elf" quality she found very attractive in a rebellious sort of way. He was so unlike all the other elves. Besides there was no one else she especially wanted to ask – everyone else seemed so dull compared to him – and, perhaps most importantly, she knew it would turn heads right and left, guaranteed to set all tongues wagging were he to be her escort.

"The ball?" he asked. "Oh – right – the ball. Um, I'm not going. Got stuff to do. Congrats."

His cheeks flushed a darker blue and he turned quickly and walked away – so quickly he failed to notice the dark green cloud forming over Trixie's emerald hair. Meanwhile many others clamored round her, both young elves and older, unattached ones, each hoping to be chosen as her escort.

That evening, with pre-ball parties and post End of Sessions revelry echoing throughout Claustown, Charcoal climbed Sugar Plum Peak*, his favorite refuge, and basked in the glow of the Midnight Sun*. He loved this spot, the highest point in town. He adored the vast, unobstructed panorama it afforded, the sparkling, prismatic fields of ice and bergs in every direction, with Claustown nestled like an insignificant little toy train village at its foot. He could almost see that wonderful shipwreck far to the south (*everything* was south of here) just at the horizon's edge.

In the summer the Peak tended to be disused, since few elves ever sat in the full sun – sunburn stings even at the North Pole. In the depths of winter, just after Delivery Season*, the populace of Claustown was generally too exhausted to do much of anything but sleep for a good month before pre-production resumed, so the Peak was pretty much his own domain then, too. Charcoal wistfully remembered last winter – his first one on the Peak - and how much he enjoyed the profound solitude and the beauty of the stars twinkling fiercely above him. He fondly remembered the first time he saw the northern lights*. He was then six months old and dazzled by their beauty. They seemed to be dancing in the sky just for him and he, a schoolboy, stood atop the Peak and slowly danced along with them – feeling at one with the winter skies, having an unaccustomed sense of belonging for perhaps the first time in his life.

That night, while he danced, he sang – a song he made up on the spot. One he'd sung many times since:

It was a sunny day in spring – the ice and snow bright glistening
Two souls together – enjoying the weather – something new was in the
offing.
A dot appeared in the sky – a bundle came from up on high,
And then before they knew – there now were three where once were two.
Another life had joined with theirs – subject of envy, scorn, and stares.
"Look at that hair …" they all said. "Look at that hair."
So one poor soul was doomed to roam – although the fault was not his
own.
Mocked and chided, despised, derided.
Different from the rest, each day another dreaded test.
"Look at that hair," they all laughed.
"Look at that hair."

Now he's learned to be alone.
His future may be far from home.
Where can he go – where can he run?
Where will he sleep when day is done?
Where can I flee? Where can I hide?
Where can I be where none deride?
Wish I could just be by myself.
Maybe hiding on a shelf,
Charcoal the Elf …

A note to the reader: Elf music is not notated. Rather, it's improvised and changes most every time a song is performed, as the lyrics are considered more important than the melody. Additionally, assuming you are human, most music you're familiar with nowadays is either diatonic or pentatonic*. Elf music comprises twenty-five tones — icosikaipentatonic* — many of them inaudible to the human ear (although dogs love the stuff), so any attempt to reproduce the melody here is futile.*

When he'd finished singing, Charcoal gazed out at the vastness. "What's out there?" he asked out loud. "Is there anywhere out there for me?"

He sighed, thought about how much he looked forward to the light show this coming winter would bring, and hoped he could, once again, lose himself in it. And that perhaps it would hurt just a bit less than last year. Just then, a shooting star streaked across the sky, leaving a sparkling trail behind it. *Oh, I wish, I wish, I wish, I wish I'd discover why I'm here,* he thought fervently.

But now, with the Midnight Sun shining across the northern latitudes, he found he couldn't escape the sounds of merriment drifting up from the town below. School had ended and uncertainty lay ahead. For as much as school was filled with pain and sorrow, at least it was a known entity, and Charcoal (he tried to convince himself) had managed to deal with it.

Now he faced a huge unknown — the future. *His* future. He felt somehow charged up and ready to do something. Something "important" — especially with the vast knowledge base he'd been building — certainly a much broader depth of knowledge about the world than any other elf now living (except, of course, for *him – Elf Number One*), but he didn't know what that might possibly be. He *did* know it wasn't simply making rocking zebras. He wanted, needed, a mission. An important mission. One that would be exciting, filled with adventure. More importantly, something to give him a sense of purpose. Something only he could do.

If only someone would tell him what it was.

* * *

With all the noise in town, when he finally returned home he found it impossible to sleep, so he slid *Ahtryvski iz vielikoy russkoy literatury* out from under his mattress and resumed thumbing through it. The book fell open to the title page of *Prestupléniye i nakazániye Fedora Dostoyevskogo*. Being an elf, of course Charcoal immediately knew that said "Crime and Punishment* *by Fyodor Dostoevsky.*" It certainly didn't sound like the title of any book he'd ever heard before. He started to read.

Crime and Punishment by Fyodor Dostoevsky confused him to no end. This story was *nothing* like the cheery holiday stories with pretty pictures his reading had been confined to until now. For that, he was grateful. He devoured it, page after page, like an elf denied cotton candy for weeks. The story was riven with confusion, paranoia, guilt, horror, and loathing. Charcoal was fascinated.

This Dostoevsky person had chosen, as protagonist, someone Charcoal sensed was an "anti-hero," a term he'd heard of before but never actually experienced until now. This contra-hero was a young male human named Raskolnikov. He didn't make toys. He didn't sing happy songs. He didn't even dance. In fact, there was pretty much nothing happy about him at all. That all seemed in some way very familiar and comforting. But he was contemplating murder. "MURDER!" exclaimed Charcoal to no one but himself. He was more than a bit shocked at the concept. He read and read until, ultimately, he fell asleep with the book in one hand, the elf-light waning in the other.

CHAPTER 7

SUMMONED

The following evening was the Great Selection Ball, the gala highlight, and the last day of Non-Delivery Season*. All that day, Distant Cousin Trixie unabashedly and pointedly stared at Charcoal as he wandered obliviously in the main square, gazing out at a cloud, a passing bird, or nothing much at all, just to avoid meeting her gaze. He could tell she was angry with him for something, but he'd already forgotten what. Their exchange of just yesterday had become ancient elfstory in his mind. All he could think about was Raskolnikov's possible pending crime.

That evening he almost bumped into her as, in full "Green Queen" regalia, complete with flowing cape and – really? – a tiara of green rhinestones (*A bit over up top,* he couldn't help but observe to himself), she was being escorted on foot by not one, *but three* besotted elves (another "first" for Claustown) toward the castle. Yes, his cousin certainly knew how to be the center of everything. And Claustown simply ate it up.

Despite her best efforts, however, it was his glaring absence from the ball that was the predominant topic of conversation for everyone's wagging tongues. He'd unwittingly upstaged the entire gala event. His no-show was on everyone's lips — and *everyone* was there … everyone except … well, you know. It was a scandal of major proportions — not a single elf could recall anyone not having attended the ball. Not anyone — not ever! This year's Great Selection Ball was destined to become legendary as a result. And fodder for absolutely delicious gossip, which continued for days afterward. Many who attended could not remember anything else about the ball — not even Trixie's spectacular debut sliding down a frozen waterfall on ice skates while twirling flaming (green) candy-cane batons. She swore she'd never forgive her cousin.

The next afternoon, as Claustown began to revive, word filtered down through the family grapevine that he had scored fabulously well in his End of Sessions exercises. His marks were the highest that year — or, in fact, any year in living memory (and elves live a *very* long time). His parents beamed; his classmates fumed. And everyone talked about the wonderful fact that none — *"Not even one!"* — of the captains had selected Charcoal for their workshop teams.

He wasn't invited to join the Toy Team (despite the rocking zebra). Electronics didn't choose him, either. His name didn't appear on the lists for Decorative Arts, Home Furnishings, Fine Jewelry, Apparel, Vehicles. Not even Socks. Although Research and Development bounced his name around briefly, they ultimately gave him the thumbs down. "Seems like a loaded cork gun," said the team captain. Even Gift and Coffee Table Books — the team where pretty much *anyone* was assured a spot — failed to add his name to their list of invitees. Score up another first for Charcoal — the first in elfstory to have failed to be selected by any team whatsoever. He seemed to be breaking records, but in all the wrong ways.

He remained the primary topic of scorn and derision by those elves who were ungenerous, judgmental and – let's face it – jealous and/or threatened by him. By those with bigger and warmer hearts, he was the subject of (very unwanted) compassion.

"Well, he certainly has got his comeuppance now!" or "Poor lost lad, he's like a reindeer-less sleigh!" they would say, depending on which side of the fence one stood.

But all through the delicious scandal rocking Claustown, he remained unheeding and immersed in his reading, poring through *Crime and Punishment* like chocolate syrup pours down a pile of butter cookies, spending almost every waking moment with book to pointy nose. Every so often a particularly startling or meaningful phrase would jump off the page.

"Pain and suffering are always inevitable for a large intelligence and a deep heart. The really great men must, I think, have great sadness on earth."

He read that phrase over and over again. "Pain and suffering ... great sadness ..." and couldn't believe what he was reading. This book was amazing. He realized he felt compassion for the (anti) hero and sympathized with him. So much more compelling a book than *The Little Choo-Choo Who Toot-Too'd.*

Their concern having reached new heights, his parents tried to engage him in conversation at meals or distract him with special treats, but Charcoal just grunted or shrugged in response. For most of the next week all anyone saw of Charcoal was his forehead, with that especially charcoal-like lock of hair curled across it. The rest of his face was buried in that old, big, beat-up, soiled, worn book, the sort of book no one in Elfdom had ever seen before – certainly not within living memory (and as you've heard before, elves live a very long time).

Despite his almost constant confusion with the content, Charcoal couldn't get enough. The more he read the more he became absorbed by the quandary that was Raskolnikov. Professor Spright was truly happy to see *anyone* reading a book once school was done. But he wasn't quite certain how he felt about *this* choice of reading material. No pictures … all those big words … so disturbing, so non-elf.

Just the bedraggled appearance of the worn-out, beat-up old book was fuel for commentary. All Elfdom was aware of his "even stranger than usual" behavior. Tongues remained wagging, heads turning from side to side, eyes and a chorus of "tut-tuts" following him wherever he went. But, as his mother, Jolly, had predicted two years (and a few days) ago, Charcoal was becoming immune to being unique. Or maybe just becoming very good at hiding his feelings. Who could tell? Perhaps not even he.

"To go wrong in one's own way is better than to go right in someone else's."

It seemed Dostoevsky had written these words just for him – as if he *knew* him. Charcoal there and then decided he simply *had* to meet this Mr. Dostoevsky. *This man is the smartest human in the whole wide world,* thought Charcoal, although in truth he had never actually met any humans and certainly couldn't speak for the entire population, of which apparently there were quite a few. And it was typical of Charcoal to resolve to do something pretty much forbidden in the Great Elf Code*. *"Elves and humans don't mix,"* as the truism goes. Shrugging his shoulders, he read on.

"Truly great men must, I think, experience great sorrow on the earth."

Charcoal wondered if only men experienced great sorrow. Did this not apply to women as well? *Does "men" mean only humans? Couldn't elves feel this way, too?* he thought. *What about animals? Can animals experience great sorrow?*

He recalled a conversation he and that singular Rudolph had had a while back in which the shiny-nosed reindeer shared how painful it had been for him in his early years when he, too, was shunned by all Claustown.

"If it hadn't been for that foggy night," he said in that nasal snuffle of his, "I might never have found my purpose in life. And look at me now – I even have my own song!"

Charcoal *so* related to what Rudolph told him. He remembered the many times he'd been shunned and mocked in his young life. But he also felt a sharp pang – not jealousy, exactly, but close. He wondered if he, too, might not have some purpose he wasn't aware of, and he pondered if someday that purpose would reveal itself for him, too. How he hoped it would. And wouldn't it be nice to have a song written about him? Preferably, a perky song with a happy ending. Or at least a positive spin.

He was practically devouring the book and had just begun the "Epilog" – a completely mysterious word.

Epilog? It sounded like some sort of a log but it didn't *look* like a log, certainly not a Yule Log, and he was completely stumped by "epi" – didn't "epi" have something to do with hair? Perhaps a "*hairy log*"? He looked it up, but the definitions "afterword" and "coda" weren't helpful at all. So "hairy log" it would remain.

Anyway, he was just beginning the "hairy log" thing one morning when his father, Chuckles, found him seated on top of Sugar Plum Peak. Huffing and puffing from the climb he managed to wheeze, "Char – I'm so glad I found you. I tried mentally calling but you didn't respond." He shot a baleful glance at "that book" and continued. "Buddy [Santa's chief assistant] stopped by the house just now looking for you. He says *Santa* wants to meet with you! He wants you at Santaschloss in half an hour."

"Santa? SANTA?! Santa Claus wants to meet with *me*??!!" Charcoal could scarcely believe his ears. "Are you sure?" Even for an elf as oblivious to outside influences as he'd become this was still a big deal.

His father said he had reacted exactly the same way, and just to be safe he double-checked with Hermey Elph, the town dentist ("you can always trust relations, you know") who confirmed that Santa, who wasn't used to being kept waiting, was expecting Charcoal at half-past ten. And here it was, already ten.

CHAPTER 8

THE MEETING

In case you couldn't tell, meeting Santa was truly the most wonderful thing any elf could aspire to. Most elves can only ever hope to meet him once – at the Great Selection Ball when they're presented to him at the end of their studies. That keeps them going for the rest of their lives (which, as you know quite well by now, is a very long time). Meeting *with* Santa was an honor so rare it could get you invited to brunches, dinners, or parties for decades thereafter. And meeting with Santa *in* his castle – "The Iceberg," or "Santaschloss" – was something to be recorded in family archives for the ages, along with s-elfies and keepsakes such as the napkin rings or teaspoons that somehow happened to accidentally fall into pockets, jacket linings, or under caps where they were later found after returning home. Charcoal knew of only three members of the Elph Clan who had ever, in all the clan's long history, actually been inside Santa's castle. Hermey, of course. He was Santa's dentist (he was *everyone's* dentist, being the only one in town); Bernard Elph, who sits on Santa's Grand Council; and Kringle Elph, who claims to anyone who will listen that many centuries ago he'd helped Santa found Claustown.

Old Kringle Elph was a legend in himself, still willing to unpoint your ears reminiscing about those early days at length — that is, if he were able to stay awake long enough to re-count the whole saga. Kringle claimed to originate in a land Down Below now called Turkey, and insists he was Santa's very first elf, the one who helped him start the whole snow-ball rolling. "Those were other days, other times, other names …" he would mutter cryptically. Whether actually true or not, doubting him was pointless. Besides, everyone begrudgingly admitted the Elph Clan was chronologically the first family of all Elfdom, and no one in the family was older than Kringle. Therefore, the other clans conceded, with coaxing, that it was "probably" true.

Charcoal wore his best outfit, looking very smart in his green unicorn-wool shorts, jacket, and cap. He had on a brand-new pair of shiny red-and-green-striped suspenders Jolly had wisely tucked away in case any of her elf-folk ever had the honor. His hair was combed — sort of — and some of the wildness of it had been tamed, although it threatened to explode back to its jungle-like self any moment. Hence the cap. Being Charcoal, he wasn't exactly on time, but he also wasn't so late it mattered — at least not much. Taking a deep breath as he approached the enormous glistening front gates, with a trembling hand he raised the huge marzipan* door knocker. But before it clanged the door shot open and one of the Wooden Soldiers caught it in mid-fall.

"Puhleeeeeez! Don't use that thing! It's so loud, every time I hear it my wooden ear drums thump for hours."

Looking him up and down and then staring fixedly at that

mop of hair poking out in every direction from under his cap he said, "Charcoal D. Elph, right? You're late."

Charcoal is considered tall for an elf, reaching the top of a polar bear's shoulder, but as he walked down the tremendous vaulted, soaring, sparkling corridor he felt downright diminutive. The ceiling seemed to vanish into the blue sky above, visible through the thin panes of ice. The soldier showed him into an enormous, vaulted room where, up a flight of twelve steps, stood Santa's glittering gold throne, studded with rock-candy jewels gleaming in brilliant colors, reflected hundreds of times in the multifaceted walls of blue ice. It was clearly designed to impress. It succeeded.

He stopped, stared around him, taking it all in. Not knowing what else to do, he stood there and waited. He tried whistling his tune just a bit, but his lips were bone dry. He realized his knees were beginning to knock together ever so slightly, and his teeth began to chatter a tad. He didn't know what to do with his hands, so he thrust them nervously in and out of his pockets, and finally decided to just hold them together. For the first time in his life, his cocky attitude failed him. *So this is what nervous feels like,* he thought. He had to think it because he couldn't speak it, not even under his breath. His voice was *that* stuck in his throat.

In one of the side walls, a small, nondescript ice-covered door he hadn't noticed swung open, creaking just slightly, and there, in a glittering frame, stood the greatest of all elves, the head honcho, the revered, idolized, one-and-only, legendary, SANTA! No fanfare reverberated through the huge columned room, but it was implicit nonetheless. Charcoal was rooted to the spot. He was much taller than Charcoal expected (having not met him at the ball he didn't attend). He was also a great deal slimmer than in his official portraits. Instead of his signature red-and-white suit, he was wearing, of all things, a pair of red Bermuda shorts with stars – no, not stars: star*fish* – all over them, and his white short-sleeved shirt was studded with green palm trees. Instead of boots his pink toes poked out of red flip-flops. Not quite what Charcoal was expecting, but he *did* look very comfortable. His famous whiskers were trimmed fashionably close to his face.

Santa looked him up and down for a few moments and thought, *So it's true about the hair. I wonder …* Then he smiled, put a finger to his lips, chuckled a bit, winked, waved his other arm and said, "Not what you were expecting, hey? You know, even Santa enjoys his downtime!"

He chuckled again and then, putting his fists to his hips he added, "Well, don't just stand there like an ice sculpture! Time's a-wasting. Come on over here." He swung the door wider to bid Charcoal enter. The young elf didn't move – couldn't move. He felt as if he were frozen (pun intended) solid. Santa beckoned and chuckled a bit harder, saying,

"Come, youngster – you've nothing to fear here. Let's settle in where it's more comfortable. I'd like to talk to you."

With that, Charcoal finally willed himself to unstick from the floor, putting one two-ton foot in front of the other. He slowly (it seemed as if years were passing) made his way toward Santa, feeling very foolish, Santa chuckling heartily all the while.

Santa ushered him into a wonderfully cozy room — low-ceilinged and snug, paneled in glowing yew, an ornate wooden mantle carved with holly leaves and berries dominating one wall. Since it was midsummer, there was no fire in the hearth, but the odor of countless fires past hung in the room, making it homey and very familiar. Overstuffed upholstered chairs and a red leather sofa completed the sense of a comfy hideaway. The room was truly warm and inviting. Charcoal's nervousness ebbed a bit as Santa motioned him to climb into one of the super-soft chairs — like sitting in a fluffy, bouncy, fleecy, rosy cloud. "Now, let's have a chat," Santa said and cleared his throat.

He looked down for a moment to gather his thoughts, during which Charcoal saw his entire brief life flash before his eyes. Santa looked up again and said, "They tell me you're having trouble fitting in, finding your place here." The twinkle in his eyes had vanished, replaced by a look of true caring. Charcoal stared blankly at him, nodding slightly, almost stupidly, mouth open. "Yet I hear your work is outstanding — potentially one of our bright future stars. So?" Slowly at first, but building momentum as his voice returned, Charcoal recounted his experiences over the past two years — his awareness of being different, the other elves treating him cruelly, teasing him mercilessly, the endless gossip, his parents' caring concern, feeling truly content only when he was alone on one of his explorations.

"Explorations?" Santa said, raising an eyebrow and looking at him gently but with noticeable interest. "What explorations?"

Feeling more like himself, Charcoal launched into tales of his forays out among the ice floes and cliffs, his various mishaps, close calls, and discoveries and, finally, his having found a treasure just the week past.

"Treasure? You've found a treasure out on the ice?"

"Well, not really a treasure if you mean gold and jewels and live gingerbread men. Actually, an old beaten-up book. But a wonderful book."

"A book? You've found a book? What sort of book?" asked Santa, leaning forward, intrigued, and perhaps just a tad on edge. Charcoal pulled the old, tattered leather-bound book out of his knapsack and showed him.

"Hmmm … Russian literature …" The book fell open at the red ribbon bookmark.

"Dostoevsky," murmured Santa, raising another eyebrow and looking at him quizzically. "You're reading Dostoevsky?"

Charcoal commenced a précis of his new favorite author – his insights, his wisdom, the profound depths of human misery that resonated so strongly for him.

"Santa, Dostoevsky says there's strife, hunger, intolerance, illness, hatred, and violence out there in the human world!" he exclaimed (he had looked each of these words up just so he was certain he knew what they meant).

"And I've *seen* it, too. On the Internet." He caught his breath. *Uh-oh, I don't think I should've said that,* he thought. *I think I just let the calico cat out of the bag.*

Another raised eyebrow from Santa. *"The Internet?"* asked the Great One. *"You've* been surfing the Internet?" he added, not sounding at all pleased.

After a moment of nervous throat clearing and frantic eye rolling while searching for a nearby escape hatch or at least a precipice he could hurl himself over, the young elf plunged in even deeper. He confessed all regarding the old abandoned basecamp he'd been frequenting – how he'd been learning much about the strange world Down Below. Santa's complexion was starting to darken. Ignoring the signs of a brewing storm, Charcoal continued:

"Santa, did you know there are millions of people suffering Down Below? There's hunger, strife, conflict. There's poverty and war. It seems the mortal world is a mess. And there are even those who say *they don't believe in you.* So many people don't put trees up in their homes or string lights and tinsel outside. We've got to do something about this! They're missing the Season of Light! They don't celebrate Yule. It's so confusing – somehow it seems so wrong for us to be sitting in Claustown painting glass balls and stringing popcorn while the human race is falling apart. We should be helping them in some way."

Santa sat quietly, listening to this torrent of thoughts until Charcoal was quite finished, and for some time after. The potential storm had passed but the darkness remained. Charcoal sat quietly himself, not quite knowing what had come over him, having never realized he felt this way before. He could see concern etched on the Great Elf's familiar countenance. He thought he even saw a tear glisten on the edge of one of his eyes.

Santa let out a deep sigh and quietly admitted, "Yes. It seems this has always been a part of the human experience, but with more and more humans every year it seems to steadily worsen. We can barely keep up with demand as it is. Public relations gets short shrift. Our message is forgotten, or worse, ignored by many. But, youngster, you don't know the fuller picture. It's not as bad as you think."

"Almost all humans celebrate something significant during the waning of the sun, and have done so for many, many thousands of years. You also don't know I appear in many different forms and have many different names – I can be myself naturally, but when I'm not Santa, I'm an old kindly witch, a scary horned creature, a fairy queen, a dwarf – even a trio of kings! And so, so many more …" (out rolled a gentle "ho, ho, ho.")

"Each of these is a part of me, and I a part of them. Put them all together and they spell S-A-N-T-A. Have you ever noticed the actual date of Delivery Day differs in many cultures, too? As early as December 6 and as late as January 6. Spreading it out certainly helps. Some cultures don't even expect gifts! Even easier for me. My lad, every year I think this will be the one when it all finally falls apart, but it never does – so far, at any rate. Of course, I don't know what I'd do without all of you elves,"—here Santa looked pointedly at Charcoal— "helping out in every imaginable way."

Charcoal gulped. He hadn't missed Santa's implication – his time could be better spent than surfing the 'net in a rusty Quonset* hut and reading Russian literature. But something had opened inside him and the words continued to roll out:

"Santa, I still think a lot of people have forgotten the wonder of Yule – they're suffering, despairing, barely managing. We must *do* something!"

He couldn't believe his own ears. Him, having the gall to sit there telling the greatest elf of all what was what. Clearly Santa wasn't expecting this, either.

"And what do you suggest *we* do?" he asked carefully.

Charcoal was even more stunned. Santa Claus – the great Santa himself – asking *him*, an adolescent elf, a nobody, one without even a workshop apprenticeship, for his opinion! He never dreamed he'd find himself in this situation, but since starting that wonderful book (although now he was wondering just how wonderful it really *was*) he realized he *had* been pondering just this – how to address Raskolnikov's dilemma on a broad level, how to reawaken the world to the true joy of the Season of Light, no matter what name they gave it or how they celebrated it. He paused for a moment, licked his lips, and plunged in with his new idea. An idea so new he was making it up as he went along.

"Send me Down Below, Santa!" he exclaimed.

Santa actually jumped with a start. Charcoal jumped with an even bigger start. Had he just said that? A moment of dead silence and then Charcoal laid out a plan he didn't even know he'd been hatching until it all came flooding out of him in a rush of words and emotion.

CHAPTER 9

THE PLAN

""There's something going on down there," said Charcoal. "I've been trying to figure it out. People on the Internet are saying right and left the world's gone crazy. No matter how bleak a picture Mr. Dostoevsky paints, it seems things Down Below are much worse in real life."

Charcoal paused, formulating words for thoughts that were only coalescing in his brain at that instant.

"I want … I want …" Charcoal's eyes suddenly grew with surprise as he realized just what it *was* he wanted.

Forging ahead he said, "With your permission, of course, I'd like to go Down Below [Santa lurched in his chair], look around, talk to people, try and grasp what they're thinking, what actually is happening, see if we can't figure out where they've gone wrong and if there's not something we might be able to do to point people back in the right direction. I don't know if it would make any difference, but I'd like to try."

The words were spilling out of Charcoal in a tidal wave now.

"I *want* to try! I know … I could assume a human shape,

go about undetected, interact, evaluate, and then present you with my data."

Charcoal stood up, erect and very serious.

"Sir, I volunteer to go Down Below and do some reconnaissance work – experience first-hand what people are dealing with and how we might help make things at least a little better for them."

With his mind spinning, his heart racing, and in complete disbelief of what had just happened, he stopped his jabbering, sat back down, and nervously waited for Santa to say something, or blast him into oblivion with a bolt of ribbon candy.

Instead, nothing. The Great Elf sat, fist to chin, brow furrowed in thought. Charcoal thought it best to sit patiently. He was confused and startled by his boldness; this turn of events having been a surprise even to himself. Not being used to prolonged conversation, he was talked out anyway.

After a deafening silence that seemed to go on for an eternity, Santa finally sighed heavily, stirred, and looked deeply into Charcoal's gray eyes with his own blue ones, not twinkling now but looking like deep, dark water.

"Charcoal …" he began, with a hint of sadness in his voice, "leave it to someone whose been terribly unhappy to want to reach out and help others. You've hit on something that's troubled me greatly for a very long time. These worries, these problems you speak of, they are not new. The human world is a strangely troubled and irrational place. One I've never fully been able to grasp despite all my years of interaction with it. You've definitely hit on something here."

"My own investigations – *yes*, yes, Santa surfs the Internet, too – have also made me feel we're losing credibility in this modern world. Humans are adrift, lost, troubled, isolated, confused. I've been feeling the same things you, in your short time on this planet, have observed so astutely. They told me you're exceptionally intelligent. I see that's true. You're quite a fellow, you are."

"I'm going to share something with you I don't think anyone else in all the North Pole knows – something that would create panic if it were known. I came into existence many, many years ago, when humankind first began thinking of the darkest season as a time for retrospection, atonement, good will, and peace to all. These thoughts and deeds created a stream of energy that combined to create – well, to create *me*. One day I wasn't; the next day I was. It was only many thousands of years later, due to circumstances too complicated to go into now, that I settled at the North Pole. One could say I was created by human kindness. Goodwill brought me – brought us all – into existence."

Charcoal gulped. Santa sat knowingly, awaiting his inevitable question.

"Well then, wha – what would happen, sir, if goodwill ceased to exist? If the evil things were to ultimately vanquish the good?"

Santa replied curtly, "Then I think *I* would cease to exist. I think we would all vanish – return to the void, to nothingness. Everything gone, as if we never were."

Charcoal trembled from head to toe.

"Now do you understand why I've kept this to myself? We must make this a solemn secret between just us two, Charcoal."

The young elf nodded gravely and said, "No one else shall ever know, sir, unless you someday allow me to share this."

For a moment they sat in silence, contemplating the thought of a world without Santa, ergo, a world without peace and goodwill. Santa shook his head and roused himself, shaking and running his hands up and down his frame as if to wipe off something unpleasant.

"Brrrrrrr... So now – no more of that. We must simply make certain it never happens. And that's that. But getting back to this plan of yours ... Let me make sure I understand. You say you want to go Down Below? Let's say, just for instance – hmmm ... two weeks. I'm certainly not comfortable sending you away longer. I'm not even comfortable with the thought of you Down Below at all. You want to take human shape, meet some of them first-hand? You must realize this could be dangerous. *Very* dangerous. You're young, inexperienced. Have you ever even seen a real live human before?"

Charcoal shook his head.

"Be warned: They are irrational and inconsistent – their emotions often override their reason. They can be your friend one moment and your enemy the next. And remember, humans have very different cultures and act in vastly different ways throughout their world. What's totally acceptable in one place can be totally unacceptable in another." He paused in thought for a moment. Looking up, he resumed.

"Charcoal, I have my doubts … I think what you're offering to do is very admirable, and honestly, could prove useful. But now that you've presented this idea, I think it would be safer if I sent one of our older, more experienced elves instead." He watched the youth carefully to assess his reaction.

Charcoal blurted out, "But, sir, who else has spent any time studying humans? As far as I know, the only elf who's ever interacted with them is your chief assistant, Buddy – and we all know what happened then. Buddy's a great elf, don't misunderstand me, but even I know about the mess he made Down Below. I may be the only one who's ever taken a scientific interest in them as a species. I've been studying them for almost six months!"

"That long, eh?" Santa chuckled that wonderful, deep chuckle. "I can't disagree with you – on *any* count! Yes, Buddy is truly singular. Let's just say his enthusiasm makes up for his … well … for his Buddy-ness. Still, total chaos does seem to follow him about. All right, we'll rule him out. As far as humans, I don't think any of us could ever truly understand them if we studied them for a hundred years, or even a thousand. I know *I* don't. Just when you think you know what they'll do, they surprise you with some other erratic behavior."

Santa fell silent again for a moment. "I'm not sure …" he shook his head sternly and stroked his short beard. Charcoal sensed the conversation was about to end. He desperately clutched at a straw.

"Sir, can I make a deal with you?" Charcoal couldn't believe his impudence, but he'd never before in his short life ever wanted to do anything as badly as this, and he had long ago learned to stand up for himself.

"Please, give me six weeks to learn everything I can about them. I'll study humans every waking moment of my day, I promise. I'll surf the Internet morning, noon, and night. I don't have anything else to do anyway." Santa nodded in understanding – naturally he knew Charcoal had not been invited into any of the workshop teams.

"At the end of my research, test me in any way you like, see what I've learned, see if you think I'm ready. Then, I'll abide by your decision, whatever it is."

Santa looked the young elf up and down. He was thinking very hard. Slowly his expression lightened. The famous twinkle reappeared in his eye.

"Charcoal, you are indeed truly unique [that word again]. Despite everything you've been through in your short life, and your solitary habits"—Charcoal wondered if Santa knew everything about every single one of them — but then again, he *was* Santa! — "you display both a remarkable personal strength and wisdom. Or, maybe it's *because* of your tough first years."

He paused again, then slapped his leg. "Fair enough. You've made your case. I agree. I'll expect you back here in forty-five days. We'll wait until then to decide if we'll proceed."

Charcoal felt as if the top of his head were going to explode.

"And now, before you go, can I give you a napkin ring or a teaspoon as a souvenir of our meeting? They seem to be very popular with visitors. They certainly seem to vanish whenever someone's here. Or perhaps a s-elfie? You'll be the envy of all."

Moments later Charcoal wandered down the huge hall in a daze (and empty-handed – napkin rings and teaspoons couldn't be further from his mind). He somehow found the Main Portal and passed through. This time the guards snapped to attention, saluting him with a respect that had been blatantly lacking when he entered. He stopped for a moment and stared. The sun was almost blinding as it sat at its highest point in the sky.

But what caught Charcoal's breath was the vast mob milling about. He'd never seen Yuletide Square so crowded at midday. Almost every elf in Claustown had somehow managed to be in front of Santaschloss at just precisely the moment Charcoal emerged into the glare. Hundreds of pairs of inquisitive eyes peered hard at him, second-guessing what might have, could have, should have, happened during his meeting with the Chief. Yes indeed, they all knew who'd been summoned to The Castle.

"There he is!"

"Do you think he's been banished to the South Pole*?"

"He seems dazed."

"What do you suppose happened?"

"Has he been reprimanded?"

"He still has the book. I can see it sticking out of his knapsack."

"I don't think he even met with Santa. I don't see a napkin ring, a teaspoon, or *any*thing!"

Ah yes … Elves can be *so* vicious.

Among the throng he spied his parents waving. Chuckles and Jolly were there waiting with a slaxi to take him home. Out of force of habit, he automatically kissed each of them as they put their arms across his numb shoulders and guided him into the open sleigh. They, too, were almost delirious with curiosity, but their concern for their son was even greater.

Chuckles finally broke through his son's daze to ask, "Is everything all right, Char?" His son nodded slightly and mumbled, so softly only they could hear.

"Wonderful!" he whispered, awe in his voice.

He sat back quietly in the sleigh all the way home, staring distantly at the back of the driver's pointed cap, still not fully grasping what had just transpired.

CHAPTER 10

Persistence Pays Off

There was quite a commotion in the abode of Chuck-les and Jolly Elph a short while later. Passersby – and there seemed to be an extraordinary number of them that day – noted raised voices and a general air of turmoil emanating from the house as they "happened to be walking by." Jolly in particular was adamantly opposed to the plan when Charcoal finally gathered his wits and explained it to them.

"No elfling of mine is going Down Below!" she insisted heatedly, to which Chuckles responded, "But dear, this could be the making of Charcoal – just the thing he's been needing to help find himself."

"Or be lost forever!" she snapped back.

And so on, and so on. We all know the routine … Most of us have been through this in some shape or form ourselves.

Meanwhile, Charcoal was already fully committed to his plan whether or not his parents agreed. He was, after all, two years old now and nearly full grown. He had camped on ice floes, explored shipwrecks, dodged polar bears, ridden a unicorn bareback, even surfed the Internet. He'd proven he could take care of himself. It was time for him to strike out on his own, either in Claustown or somewhere else, wherever that might be, and he was eager to get started.

Still, he had never seen his parents disagree so completely or argue so heatedly. He could see tiny beads of moisture on the living room walls, as if their home were beginning to melt. But in the end, he knew it was ultimately his own decision to make and his mind was set firmly. He was "going down" as they say at the North Pole. That is, *if* he passed Santa's test – and he knew it would be a tough test. It would make rocking-zebra construction seem like a stroll on Sugar Plum Peak.

And so, it was finally settled. Despite her apprehension, Jolly ultimately conceded to Chuckles's calm persuasion and Charcoal's immovable determination. True to the agreement, Charcoal spent the next weeks studying humans voraciously. Santa arranged for a direct Internet signal straight into the Elph home. Morning, noon, and night, Charcoal thought humans, he dreamed humans, he showered humans, he ate humans (well, almost).

Although not at all pleased, Jolly did her best to be supportive. She didn't like the prospect of what her son might be dealing with – didn't like it at all – but she didn't dare question Santa. That would be unimaginable. And, on some level, she didn't feel she could challenge Charcoal, either. He was showing a new focus, a grounding and self-assurance she'd never seen before. She liked it. She might not like this project, but she liked the effect it seemed to be having on her son.

Chuckles, on the other hand, was thrilled his son was going on such an important and fabulously dangerous mission.

What he didn't like was the enforced secrecy of it all. *Top* secrecy. Totally hush-hush. It pained him not to finally be able to brag about his son, especially after all the ribbing he'd endured himself for the past two years. He struggled to keep from revealing Char's project, especially in an incautious moment.

Luckily, the rest of Claustown decided Charcoal had been severely disciplined by Santa. This explained his sudden disappearance from his usual haunts. He was no longer idling away his time reading that awful-looking old book on top of Sugar Plum Peak. Claustown Security noticed he'd stopped sneaking out beyond the city walls. In fact, he was no longer seen anywhere – it seemed he had simply shut himself up at home, not coming out at all. More fuel for delicious gossip. It seemed that Charcoal, to everyone's satisfaction, had been totally grounded by their esteemed leader. All that was necessary for the gossip-mongers was to invent the severity of his punishment. As more time passed with nary a sign of the one-of-a-kind mop-top, speculation increased.

"I hear he's not even here. He's been expelled from Elfdom," said one of the Faeries.

"I hear he's been banished to the South Pole penguin camps," said one of the Sprights.

Many others concurred that Chuckles and Jolly Elph had simply had enough and grounded him indefinitely. All agreed it was time he finally learned to behave like a respectful, and respectable, elf should.

"And not a moment too soon. Too late, if you ask me!" said grumpy Great Aunt Nixie Pixie to anyone who would listen.

It was apparent Jolly was avoiding the neighbors, too, grocery shopping at odd times and walking their pet seal in remote parts of town or only after dark – coming a bit earlier each day now. Chuckles, on the other hand, still regularly frequented his favorite pub, The Hanging Mistletoe, but his behavior seemed atypical, too. Once or twice, while in his cups, he hinted that things weren't as they appeared.

"Sshomeday there might be sshome reck'nin' at hand and sshome bad-mouthin' to be accounted fer," he slurred.

Luckily, he had enough presence of mind to hush up at that point and not spill the jellybeans. No one tended to take him seriously when in his cups anyway, and no one pressed him to explain what he meant. Besides, the truth was almost never as good as malicious gossip, and this gossip was simply too scrumptious to let the truth get in its way.

The whole situation was a golden opportunity to bad-mouth the Elphs. "They've certainly had *their* comeuppance, that clan has!" exclaimed a passing gremlin, who had never forgiven the family for an imagined slight a few hundred years ago, which hadn't happened at all but was an excellent excuse to hold a grudge.

"Full of themselves. I've always said so. This'll knock them down a few pegs. Glad to see it," he mumbled contentedly to himself as he trudged off.

* * *

But there was one in Claustown who wasn't accepting things as they appeared. Trixie Pixie, although only a very distant cousin (as we've established), seemed to have inherited the same smarts as Charcoal. She heard the talk but wasn't buying it.

This behavior isn't like Char at all, she thought. *Something's up.*

So, one day, after apprenticeship training (she'd been placed in haute couture), she marched up to the Elphs' front door and knocked on it smartly. Jolly answered.

"I'd like to see Cousin Charcoal, please," said Trixie.

"Well now, dear, you know, he's just not been himself lately. We think he's contracted something on one of those exploration things of his. Might even be walrus fever*. Very contagious, you know! Best to just let him be for a while longer." And the door shut before she could say another word.

Trixie wasn't having it. Cousin Jolly didn't appear in the slightest concerned that anyone might have been exposed to anything. And Cousin Chuckles hadn't much changed his routine, either, being almost as gregarious as ever. Neither of them looked ill. In fact, they both appeared suspiciously well. Clearly something was up. *Something no one was supposed to know about.* Burning with curiosity, Trixie returned after dark. She was an excellent shape-shifter (she was excellent at practically everything) and changed herself into an icicle hanging directly over Charcoal's window. What she saw made her nearly crack in two.

There was Charcoal, looking just as healthy as ever, although his signature hair was an even more tousled overgrown mess than usual. His desk was covered with papers, photographs, some sort of large drawing with X's and O's and arrows all over it and – wait – what was that? A computer!

What is Charcoal doing with a computer? she thought furiously.

The only computer Trixie had ever seen in all of Claustown was in Delivery Central Control downtown, and even she was not permitted to so much as touch it. Computers would make it very easy for Down Below to connect Up Top*, and no elf wanted that! "Dear Santa" letters were where the line was drawn as far as all were concerned. And besides, what good would owning a computer be when elves already have everything they could possibly use? So then, *why* did Charcoal have a computer? The mystery was growing by leaps and bounds. So was her curiosity.

Just then she saw Jolly enter with a tray containing a double-decker marzipan and nougat sandwich and a cup of hot cocoa with peppermints. Icicle Trixie simply couldn't figure this out. Clearly *something* important was happening having nothing whatsoever to do with all the stories flying around Claustown. Nor did it involve walrus fever. She was more determined than ever to find out the truth.

Trixie returned the next day. And the next. And the next. Her own parents took no notice, as she was always out and about rehearsing or planning or doing something fabulous, so this was usual behavior for her. She stubbornly and punctually returned to the Elph abode every day after training until Jolly and Chuckles would just look at the clock on their chimney, mosey up to the front door and wait for her knock. Their respect for this sparkling, verdant young elf was growing. More importantly, Charcoal's respect for her – already great – grew incrementally each time she knocked. He certainly admired her persistence and determination (and clearly he'd been forgiven for the Green Queen debacle). It set him to thinking, and he had an idea. He composed an email to the Boss (telepathy was too informal) – the first he'd written since the project began. Or ever, for that matter.

Sir - Forgive this unscheduled communication. I don't doubt you already know my distant cousin Trixie Pixie has been coming by every day insisting on seeing me. It's been more than a week and shows no signs of stopping. I have an idea, which I'd like to talk over with you if I may.

He hit "send" and awaited a response. He didn't wait long.

Within moments his computer beeped and there online, face-to-face, was the Great One. This was only the second time Charcoal had ever seen him up close, but somehow, he felt they'd been in constant contact.

"Yes, Charcoal, what is it?" asked Santa.

As if he didn't already know, thought Charcoal.

He described Trixie's persistence, her daily visits, her insistence on seeing him. He wondered if here, perhaps, was another who might be able to carry out the mission alongside him, providing mutual cover, support, and perspective on the info being gathered and how to deal with anything untoward that might present itself Down Below. Santa listened, nodded, listened some more. Charcoal noted he didn't seem especially surprised at the young elf's idea. It almost seemed as if he'd been expecting something of the sort. Santa interrupted only once:

"You realize you've been at your study several weeks now, whereas your cousin would be starting at square one? Time *is* of the essence here if we're going to get you Down Below and back before it's too late in the year. Do you think you can get her up to speed quickly enough?"

Charcoal admitted he didn't know but was willing to give it a shot. He didn't even know if Trixie was willing to join the project.

"Do you think you can trust her with our secret if she doesn't want to participate?" asked Santa. But they both already knew the answer.

A moment later it was confirmed. An odd, insistent tapping on the window interrupted them. Charcoal glanced up just in time to see a rather greenish icicle change itself into Distant Cousin Trixie. In person. She'd been there the whole time and had heard everything. Charcoal opened the window.

"You may as well come in," he said.

Trixie climbed in, dusted herself off, and made an extremely polished and graceful curtsy to the white-bearded man (his beard noticeably longer now) on the computer monitor.

"Nice to see you again, sir," she said with a graciousness belying her youth.

"Likewise, Your Majesty the Green Queen," chuckled the Elf of All Elves, eyes twinkling a brilliant blue. Charcoal stared, mouth wide open. It seemed very suspiciously as if this had all been planned in advance.

CHAPTER 11

GETTING ACQUAINTED

Trixie proved a quick study. A *very* quick study. No surprise, really, since she'd been spying on him – as a cloud, a puff of chimney smoke, a shiny glass ornament (green, of course), a doodad on his shelf, and, as you know, an icicle – ever since Jolly shut the door in her face that first day she came by. She'd been eavesdropping – sometimes literally – for almost as long as Charcoal had been studying and was almost as prepared as he. Charcoal was secretly relieved at the idea of having a companion on this, his most dangerous exploration. He saw the value of another set of eyes and another brain to work through the plan that was beginning to hatch itself. And what a plan it was …

"The idea, as I think you already know," explained Charcoal, "is to interact with humans Down Below. We need to figure out the best way to gauge just how far off track they've drifted."

"Sort of a Yule Tool," responded Trixie.

She obviously thought it was the funniest thing she'd ever heard and fell in a heap on Charcoal's faux polar bear rug, convulsed in laughter. She was one of the very few elves Charcoal could tolerate, but there were times …

He bit his lip, which yummily still tasted of the chocolate-chip-and-sugared-mint sandwich he had just finished, rolled his eyes, and ignored the remark. He cast her his most direful glance – the one he'd once used to stop a charging bull walrus in his tracks.

"Look, are we going to be serious about thjis or aren't we?"

"Right, right," giggled Trixie, obviously tickled pink (which was definitely *not* her color) over this zinger. She struggled to pull herself together again. Suddenly Charcoal had serious doubts about her. It wouldn't be the last time.

"Can we please get back on track here? We need to prepare a course of action, a plan, and then stick to it if it works. If it doesn't, we'll need to have some alternatives ready. One thing is already clear – *no more terrible jokes!*" exclaimed the exasperated elf.

Trixie sighed a deep sigh. It was now her turn to roll her eyes (*It was too funny, was too!* she thought). But she did her best to look contrite.

"Yes, Char – you're right. This is serious business and we need to act seriously."

She then made a face that was such a perfect imitation of Charcoal's usual dour demeanor it nearly set her off again when she saw her reflection in the ice mirror on the wall.

It was her turn to bite her lip. She said, "So tell me what

you're thinking of doing."

Charcoal launched into a summary of all that had happened, including an abbreviated rendition of his finding "the Book," how it confirmed his opinions about the misery of life (Trixie filed *that* in a special compartment in her brain) and motivated his current project.

"So we're trying to save the entire mortal world from itself?" she asked, in total earnestness. Charcoal was beginning to think this collaboration was a truly bad idea.

"Ugh – Trix. Let's keep this foremost in our heads: We are on a *scouting mission*. A reconnaissance assignment to gather general information and return to Claustown. That's it. Nothing more. We're just going to gather information. To try and compile some insight into why humans do the things they do, and if they have truly lost the essence of Yuletide."

Something in the tone of his voice caused Trixie in turn to wonder if this was such a good idea. *I think he's* enjoying *the thought of all those unhappy people,* she thought. For the first time in her life, Trixie Pixie experienced pessimism. Such was the power of Charcoal D. Elph!

Despite her misgivings, she was fascinated – she reveled at the chance for a real adventure as well as an opportunity to try and crack the shell of that frustrating cousin of hers. She really liked Char, in a way she couldn't explain. No one she knew confused her more than he. Everyone around her seemed to worship her; treated her as the greatest thing since electricity replaced candles on Yule trees. Everyone except Charcoal, that is. He caused her to question herself. He kept her off balance and engaged in a way the others couldn't. He certainly wasn't like anyone else she knew. But then again, he was unique. *As am I!* she thought, peeved for having admired someone other than herself.

"So what are you thinking of doing?" she repeated, a bit of an edge to her voice.

Charcoal explained the details of his plan. He wanted to travel to different parts of Down Below – "They're called countries" – and observe how different cultures celebrated the year-end Yuletide.

"What do you mean 'different cultures?'" asked Trixie. "Do you mean humans aren't all the same?"

The only ones she'd ever encountered, and it nearly scared the lollipops off her necklace, was a team of Arctic explorers. She had impetuously wandered away from her Nature Study field trip and stumbled upon some scientists chipping away at the ice. *Human* scientists. Thinking super quickly, she was able to transform herself into a snow drift before they saw her, but it was a very close call. The upside was she had her first – and so far only – chance to observe humans up close.

Not that there was much to observe. Of course, she knew what they looked like. She'd seen them in picture books at the Saint Nicholas Memorial Free Library, but there was very little she could see resembling "human" on these particular creatures. She had heard they came in different colors, too, just like elves, but all she saw were vaguely humanoid shapes encased in lumpy, shiny, silver attire. She ultimately realized they were actually inside some sort of protective gear – which amazed her completely. Why was it they seemed determined *not* to expose themselves to the splendid gale blowing just then, as if there was something wrong with snow and ice blowing through your hair making it all stand straight back in frozen glory?

Each of them had a funny little rectangular, brightly colored image on their chests – some with letters, some with stars; some with pretty pictures, and one with a hammer and something resembling a crescent moon on a handle. Remembering the close call now, she suddenly realized these were identifying patches indicating which culture – um, country – each of these humans belonged to Down Below. *I think those were some sort of identifying flags,* she thought. *Like our clan banners,* she mused, as the light of realization grew brighter in her head. Her intelligence delighted her.

Any lingering doubts she might have had about this "adventure," as Char kept calling it, evaporated. She was going to see amazing things and have experiences probably no one in Claustown – not even that whacky giant-sized Buddy, who'd actually *lived* with a mortal family for a while – had ever had before. She would be honored and applauded by the other elves even more than she already was. This was too good to pass up. She only hoped Char wasn't going to spoil it all by being such a grump.

"Um – EXCUSE me …" Char's voice cut through her reverie. "Did you hear a word I said, or am I just adding humidity to the room?"

"Uh – right – sorry," said Trixie. "I was so fascinated by what you were saying I sort of went into a trance."

Smart move. She could see Char was flattered rather than peeved. But now she really needed to pay attention.

"So – as I was saying," he continued pointedly, "I'm hoping to visit and compare several cultures Down Below. My research indicates there are marked differences from one area to another. Totally different customs, even different languages."

Trixie snorted. "You mean people from one place don't even speak the same way people from another place do?" She was amazed. "How can anyone understand anyone else?"

"Well, it appears they often don't," responded Charcoal. "I'd like to examine this to see if it's part of the problem. From what I've seen on the Internet (Trixie was *fascinated*), it seems people from these different countries often don't even *trust* each other, forget about understanding each other. This can lead to extremes – even armed conflict, what they call 'war.' There are a couple of those going on right now. I suspect all this misunderstanding and strife may be contributing to the decline in Yuleness."

"OK – so what's your plan?" she asked. She had a feeling she'd asked this question before. She also had a feeling this was going to be something carols would be written about in the future. Imagine, *her* – in a carol!

Charcoal stepped in front of the large, weird, squiggly no-shape drawing hanging on the wall. He had a long peppermint stick in his hand. He used it to point out specific blobby shapes on this drawing. Trixie realized with a flash this wasn't just bad art. She knew what this drawing was – she had heard of this in Nature Study. This was … What was the word? A *map*. Right! A map of the very planet they lived on.

She studied it carefully and noted the different sizes and shapes of the blobs. *That must be Down Below … Those must be continents,* she thought. *Or is it countries? It's one of those words. Begins with a "C." Anyway, that's where the humans live.* Geography had not been her best subject in school.

She looked at the top of the chart and couldn't help but chuckle. Whatever exactitude was used to portray the rest of the planet, she could see the northernmost regions were grossly in error. *They don't have Claustown charted,* she realized, and smirked. And the planet, which she had always heard called simply "Down Below," appeared to be called "Terra" on this map. With her ability to translate any language into Elvish (a skill she didn't know she had until just this moment) she thought, *Why do they call it "Earth" when it's obviously much more water?*

"Ahem." Charcoal's voice brought her attention back to the moment once again.

"Is this going to continue ceaselessly?" he growled. "You're not listening to a word I'm saying." He put the peppermint stick pointer down with a smack that shattered it. "I don't think this is going to work out."

Trixie begged him to forgive her. "I promise I'll be better," she said. "This is just all so new, so *exciting*. There's so much to know. I'm having trouble absorbing all this. I promise it'll stop."

Charcoal rolled his gray eyes and looked very annoyed.

"I'm not at all convinced being a team is going to work," he said. "You're too mercurial." Charcoal *loved* that word. He'd recently learned it, having read it in one of those Russian stories, but had never had the chance to use it, since he spoke with others so rarely. It was totally the perfect word.

"I'm sorry – for Nick's sake! How many times do I have to say it?" said Trixie, getting testy herself. "Just give me a chance to absorb all this and you'll see. I'll be much better – I *promise*."

"Well … I'll give you just one more chance," he said. "There are two weeks left before I – umm, *we* – present our plan to Santa. So we need this to gel solidly really soon."

Trixie nodded energetically. She would've batted her eyes at Char if she thought that would work, but it never had before so she didn't bother. She waited for him to cool down and didn't say another word. He talked a while longer, tracing invisible lines across the blobs with a fresh pointer. He droned on about prevailing winds, something called time zones, and climate variability (whatever *that* was).

Finally, he leaned against the edge of the desk and said, "OK – let's call it quits for tonight. This has been a really intense day. I think we both need to get some shut-eye. We'll resume in the morning. But I'm warning you …"

Trixie flashed him her absolutely best smile and hugged him as if he were the sweetest, most adorable holiday puppy ever created, while Charcoal squirmed.

"You'll see – by tomorrow I'll have absorbed all this and I'll be much better. I—"

"I know, you promise!" said Charcoal.

She gathered up her things, took a last gulp of hot chocolate, and prepared to leave. Suddenly, on impulse, she turned and gave Charcoal a great big kiss on his cheek, catching him totally by surprise. Charcoal gasped and took a giant leap backward.

"And no more of THAT!" he exclaimed, rubbing his cheek as if it had been smeared with seal slime. Trixie bounced out of his room. "See you tomorrow!"

Charcoal was less convinced than ever. *This is a bad idea,* he thought.

CHAPTER 12

BECOMING A TEAM

After this rough start things improved quickly. Trixie had been excused from apprenticeship training by a mysterious request from the Boss himself. It soon became clear to all in Claustown that Trixie had disappeared as completely as her cousin, although no one put the two facts together and certainly didn't guess they were working on a project together. Clever Trixie devised a slew of disguises each morning as she walked to the Elphs' home. It was good practice for her shape-shifting but was also simply fun tricking her neighbors. She was especially fond of whiffs of mist and snow squalls.

The usually wagging tongues of the town were, for once, silent other than to speculate where she might be. It was agreed whatever it was, given Trixie Pixie's dazzling appearance and personality, it was "something important." That it might involve her cousin Charcoal occurred to no one. That it was probably of huge significance to Claustown no one doubted. Everyone knew Trixie Pixie was destined for greatness. One could tell simply by looking at her. For once, all the town gossips could do was to wait, watch and wonder. It drove them all half crazy. Meanwhile, the sane half gossiped about each other, watching, wondering, and waiting with bated breath.

With the initial excitement behind her, Trixie was able to calm down and focus. She rapidly became the creative collaborator Charcoal had hoped for. She grasped every nuance of the plan as it evolved, contributing much to it as well. Charcoal's doubts and concerns vanished. He found himself almost enjoying her presence. Almost.

One day, deep into their investigations, they agreed it was time for a "rehearsal," to see how well they worked in the field under real-life circumstances. They decided to venture into Polar Bear Territory (the PBT). It would be a trial run to assess their ability to work together in challenging circumstances. They would report back to Santa as to the outcome of the experiment and adjust for the "real project" as needed.

Part of the rationale in choosing the PBT for their trial run was that humans could often be found there studying the magnificent creatures. Apparently, they'd taken a great interest in the white-furred, majestic but dangerous beauties. The likelihood of confronting both a threatening native carnivore *and* an equally scary (and much more unpredictable) human was high. This would be an ideal testing ground for the cousins.

It wouldn't be the first time elves had interacted with polar bears (not always with a positive outcome), nor would it be the first time for dealing with humans, but it could very well be a first for encountering both simultaneously. They could kill two trolls with one snowball, as the saying goes.

Charcoal and Trixie had both done very well in Wilderness Training (no surprise there). Although Trixie had no actual endurance experience, Charcoal was seasoned at non-Claustown survival (by choice) and felt confident he could deal with pretty much anything the exploration might throw at them. The night before their departure, bags packed, provisions counted and recounted, simulations run and rerun, Charcoal settled into a deep and contented sleep. It had been a while since he'd been out of the house and living by his own wits, away from the pressures, expectations, and judgments of bustling, noisy, claustrophobic, nosey Claustown.

His dream of going Down Below seemed on the verge of coming true. Going "explorationing" with someone else was a new factor and an unexpected twist, and would present its own problems and experiences, but he was confident Trixie could keep up with him and bring her own formidable assets to the adventure. He found himself actually looking forward to the companionship of a joint adventure.

At the same moment, halfway across Claustown, Trixie was experiencing very different emotions. She was excited. More so than she'd ever been before. More than she'd even been as Green Queen. Generally, she took things in stride. It all came so easily for her. She asked herself if she was nervous, having never been nervous before despite always being the center of attention wherever she went, but she decided *excited* was really the word for it.

Although she was *the* up-and-coming young celebrity of Claustown and was expected by everyone "to amount to something," she had never experienced anything remotely resembling what was about to happen in a few hours. She would be outside her comfort zone. Whenever she had ventured beyond the town gates, it was always with a group of her peers and instructors (except for that one close call). She had rarely been out of sight of the towers and chimneys of her familiar and adoring world. Now she was about to step into a wilderness she could barely imagine. One where her looks, charm, and glamor, for the first time in her life, amounted to nothing. She felt confident and prepared – mostly – but was *very* glad Charcoal would be with her.

Char is my favorite elf in all the world. There's no one else I trust as I do him, she thought as she finally drifted off to sleep.

Early next morning, the bottom of the late-summer sun was just scraping the horizon, causing the drifts, bergs, and snow-covered hills and crags to sparkle and glisten in a prism of colors. Two intrepid young elves would soon be in the midst of it.

Charcoal woke and sprang out of bed, feeling ready for anything the next few days might bring. Telepathically he reached out to a bleary-eyed, groggy, and barely awake Trixie. He had never thought of asking her if she was a "morning elf" before, but he found out now.

With a sigh he said to his folks at breakfast, "I hope this isn't going to be a problem. She needs to be in top form at any moment if a crisis presents itself."

Jolly hid her own nervousness, smiled, and served her son another helping of candied almond cakes. "Now, Charcoal," she said, "I'm sure your cousin will rise to any occasion which presents itself. You know, she doesn't have your experience, but she'll catch on. She's a very clever elf. Most importantly, I think you're pretty much ready for anything, and you won't be so far away you can't just call the whole thing off if you need to."

"NEVER!" cried Charcoal, jumping up from the toadstool* he'd been sitting on. "I'll go it alone if I must, but this project is *happening* no matter what mess she makes of it!"

Jolly smiled quietly and continued pouring hot cocoa into his insulated Santa mug. It hadn't been easy having a son so different from the others, but she knew she ultimately wouldn't have it any other way. She also believed a benevolent eye would be watching them both the entire time they were out in the wilderness. She was confident the Great Elf wouldn't let them take such a colossal risk without protecting them in some manner.

Soon, she and Chuckles were standing at their front door waving and smiling (of course worried to death inside, as any parent would be) as Charcoal blithely walked out the front gumdrop gate, turned to his right, and headed down the lane to meet up with his cousin as planned. There were slightly parted curtains and blinds in the cottages all around, as neighbors peeked and pondered what new situation "that troublemaker Charcoal Elph" was about to get himself into. Oh yes – with his sudden reappearance there would definitely be talk in town today. The window-peepers were destined for more frustration because his re-disappearance was imminent. As he turned the corner and strolled out of sight, Charcoal dissolved into a wisp of vapor, one heading for the corner of

Starswept Lane and Sparkle Avenue, the agreed meeting place with his cousin. The test run had begun.

CHAPTER 13

A Near Miss

Nature was smiling broadly that morning, spreading a welcome mat for the two adventurers. It was a stunningly beautiful day – the kind of morning in which one stops, looks at the sky, inhales deeply, and continues on one's way with a smile and a bounce. A truly observant elf would've noticed two unlikely wisps of vapor streaking through the town, one almost hopping and skipping, the other moving steadily, both oddly moving against the wind as they neared the town gates. But it was too wonderful a morning to take much note. Besides, any elf worth their salt would've been busy peering into their neighbors' windows.

Once securely through the gates and out of sight of the town, Charcoal and Trixie resumed their elvish forms. Shape-shifting was taxing. They knew they'd gain strength and endurance with continued practice, but right now they needed to conserve their energies for what unknown challenges awaited them in the wilderness over the next few days. Best to stay in their natural forms as often as possible for now. Still, Trixie leapt, wheeled, flipped, and danced through the sun-sparkling snow, and even Charcoal approximated – for him – something resembling good humor.

Anyone watching would've known at once these were two excited young elves. And someone *was* watching. Or, I suppose I should say some*thing* … If they'd been paying more attention (and why weren't they?), they'd have noticed a mound of snow – a snowdrift, actually – which seemed to be following them, moving at exactly the same speed as the two adventurers, stopping when they stopped, turning when they turned. A casual observer would have thought it merely a typical, albeit large, snowdrift, windblown and ever-shifting. But the wind – more a breeze today – was blowing in the opposite direction. This snowdrift was apparently moving with purpose. As the day progressed, the two elves headed towards Polar Bear Territory, accompanied by the odd, unnoticed snowdrift.

Polar bears are magnificent, but fierce, creatures. They're intelligent, strong, cunning – and at this time of year, hungry. The fish were running and a pack of *Ursus maritimus* were gorging while they could, storing up fat for the long winter ahead. The fish were scrumptious, but just the same, a change in the menu would be nice. A couple of tender young elves would be a delicious change of pace.

One especially large bear picked up a scent she hadn't smelled in quite some time. *Sweet,* she thought. *But not sweet the way some sea creatures are. I've tasted this sweet before but not for a very long time. I liked it.*

She recalled once, many years prior, when she had sneaked up on an unsuspecting group of creatures. Odd creatures because they walked on two limbs. They were neither very tall nor very small, and slender – definitely not fattened up for the winter. But a delicious odor emanated from them – a sort of sugary-spicy aroma. Now, you or I would have described it as peppermint mixed with cinnamon and ginger, but a polar bear wouldn't know such things. However, it was entrancing and seductive.

This polar bear had been overcome by this wonderful scent and needed to learn what this odor tasted like, so she stalked this group of creatures cautiously and patiently until one of them separated itself from the others. As the creature bent over to pick something up, she pounced and was startled to see the others dissolve into mist, snow, and puddles. But the incautious one was caught in her jaws and became a treat she never forgot. Although it had an odd covering that was entirely indigestible, her massive, sharp claws peeled it off the creature with little effort. What was underneath was skimpy, but delicious! Now she smelled that scent again. And it was getting stronger, as was her craving.

Off in the distance she caught sight (polar bears have excellent vision) of the source of that enticing reminder – two of those same strange gangly creatures, a bit smaller than the last one she had feasted on, but bewitching nonetheless. One of them leapt and wheeled and spun, all the while making a good deal of noise – a sort of high-pitched, squealing sort of sound, which kept changing pitches. The other, a bit larger, was more sedate and vocalized in a lower and softer cadence – almost a grunt. The creatures seemed completely unaware of her. It was very odd. But *very* compelling.

"Isn't this wonderful?" squealed Trixie. "Oh Char – this is so exciting."

"Shhhhhhh, Trixie, lower your voice!" said her cousin cautiously. He was sure she could be heard all the way back in Claustown. "Calm down! There's no telling what's out here. We're deep in the PBT. No sense in calling attention to ourselves."

"Oh Char – that's *so* like you!" was the response. "There's not a soul around and we haven't a care in the wor—"

A sudden roar and a blinding blur of white interrupted her as the bear charged them. Total confusion. Claws flashing. Teeth snapping. Trixie screaming. Charcoal so startled he tumbled headfirst into the snow. Luckily, an elf scream isn't like the scream of, for instance, a human being. In human terms, it's sort of a combination of a high-pitched train whistle, screeching automobile brakes, and fingernails scraping a chalkboard. Not that an elf would describe it this way. To them a scream was simply a scream. To a polar bear it was completely startling, and Trixie, in the state of euphoria she had just been in, let loose with an extra-loud, extra-high, extra-penetrating, extra-confusing scream, stopping the bear in its tracks, stunned.

Trixie cried out to her cousin. "Char, Char! Are you all right?" And with that she began to spin – faster and faster – pulling up snow all around her, creating a very localized snow squall, further confusing the bear.

By this point Charcoal was back on his feet and saw what his resourceful cousin was doing. He clapped his hands and the thunder he created was so disorienting the bear turned and fled in a panic. *No* snack was worth this aggravation. As she fled it seemed a mound of snow propelled her, pushing her forward. She found this even more disconcerting. It would be a long time before she'd try those creatures as a side dish again. But the two adventurers, too shaken to take note, both sank to their knees in the snow, panting and trembling all over.

"Whew!" said a very shaken Trixie. Her two hearts were pounding in counterpoint and her breathing was short and jerky as she struggled to her feet. "Are you all right?"

Charcoal nodded yes. "You?"

Trixie nodded. As Charcoal rose, he looked at her with all the gravitas he could muster – which was substantial. She pouted.

"You realize how close our project came to ending just now? Trixie, what were you thinking?"

Trixie kicked at the snow, looking sullen and crestfallen. She'd never been scolded before. It was difficult to bear. "I would argue with you," she said, "but you're right. I put both our lives in terrible danger just now."

She looked into Charcoal's eyes deeply – so deeply he had to try hard not to flinch. "I'm so, *so* sorry," she sighed.

She held her left hand up and made the elf sign of honor, touching her thumb and smallest finger together, the other two fingers forming a V.

"I swear nothing like this will ever happen again. I was too excited. I was out of control. But believe me, I've learned my lesson. And how! From now on the excitement will be internal. Cool, calm, and control are the only things I'll manifest," she said, oozing coolth, calmth, and controlth.

Charcoal, despite everything, had to smile — or what passed as a smile for him. "Trixie, I was just about to call this whole thing off, but there's something that makes me believe you — in spite of everything. Let's chalk this one up as a lucky — a *very* lucky — near miss. A learning experience that narrowly skirted being a horrible disaster."

Trixie could've sworn she saw a tear welling up in his eye — or maybe it was just an ice crystal. At any rate, she was deeply relieved, in several ways. That her foolishness hadn't resulted in anything worse than a very frightening experience and a torn sleeve; that she had learned a valuable lesson; that Charcoal had enough faith in her to continue when he could've easily called the entire thing off; and that together they had saved themselves from a savage polar bear attack with basically no worse an outcome than a heightened pulse rate and a session with a needle and thread. And wounded pride.

Trixie had learned some things about herself, too: That she had a deep well of bravery she never knew existed until today — she'd never needed it before — and that she possessed an innate sense of resourcefulness she knew she could rely on in the future. There was now no doubt she could think clearly and effectively in a crisis.

Still, she knew it would be difficult falling asleep tonight. And falling asleep was the next order on the agenda. The Arctic day would soon be waning. By now a campsite should've been selected, their tents pitched, and their gear stowed. They needed to get a move on to set up camp before what passed for darkness at this time of the year set in, and in this region, lanterns were completely out of the question. They didn't dare draw any more attention to themselves than absolutely necessary. They moved quickly but stealthily.

And *very* quietly!

CHAPTER 14

HUMANS

Despite what they'd been through, they both slept deeply and soundly. Come morning, it was a simple task to heat some marzipan soup and hot chocolate for breakfast using the old elf trick of rubbing their hands together and generating heat. Elves truly appreciate comfort and coziness – their lovely homes reflect that – but they're highly adaptable creatures when they need to be. They can survive almost anywhere (as we will learn). One thing was certain – there would be no more histrionics to attract hungry polar bears in the future. Or a hungry anything else, for that matter.

Both Charcoal and Trixie kept all senses on high alert as they struck camp. The group of bears so busy fishing (and hunting) yesterday had moved on and there were no other denizens of the Far North in sight. Delving deeper into the wilderness, they munched on high-energy cinnamon-coated molasses bars, and the morning passed without event. After several hours of walking, Trixie, almost giving in to her need for constant stimulation, began to wonder if anything at all would happen. Charcoal, on the other hand, plodded steadily along, seemingly knowing exactly where he was headed. He would stop, look, get his bearings, and then move on, looking for all the world like an elf on a mission – with a specific destination in mind.

The sun had just passed its zenith when a bored Trixie spotted their objective. There in the distance, about a half hour's walk ahead, were strange bumps – for lack of a better word – in the snow. Regularly spaced, long, arched bumps. They didn't look natural.

She noticed Charcoal had slowed down, moving ahead more cautiously, in a crouch, alert and apprehensive. He signaled her to do the same. *Now's my chance to finally check out a functioning base camp,* he thought.

As they approached, they became aware of strange sounds. Definitely non–polar bear. Something different. Voices. Not clear, crisp elfin voices. These voices were muffled and gruff, as if they were bottled up inside something. And then Trixie spotted them – the same type of odd-looking humans she'd seen the year before when she'd had that close call. And suddenly Charcoal was nowhere to be seen.

Frantically, she called to him telepathically. *Char, where are you?*

Just to your right. Look down.

And there, sure enough, in the bottom of a gully was her cousin. She'd never seen him like this ever before.

What's up?

Charcoal jerkily motioned for her to climb down the gully. He looked her straight in the eyes. She could see he was shaking a bit. His pupils were dilated, his eyes wide with apprehension.

"I've never seen humans before," he whispered nervously.

Trixie tossed her head. "What are you talking about? You've been studying humans for weeks now."

"Yes," he replied, "but those were just images on the screen. I've never actually seen a real, live, breathing, in-the-flesh, unpredictable human being before."

Trixie realized this was a milestone moment for her cousin. She also realized he had not a clue what to do next. Clearly, he had headed straight for this expedition camp by choice but hadn't thought of what to do once he arrived.

Now it was Trixie's turn to take charge. "Humans aren't such a big deal," she said, tossing her head.

Charcoal looked at her in wonder. "You mean … you've encountered them before?"

Trixie had never told another living elf of her own adventure last year. She sensed it would create a furor in Claustown and had studiously avoided mentioning it to anyone. It seemed best. Even her own parents didn't know. But now she told her experience to Charcoal in detail. He listened in awe. When her tale ended, they both sat on their haunches for a few moments, she reliving it, he imagining what it must have been like.

"So, what do we do now," they both said to each other at the same moment. They would have laughed if they dared.

Instead, there was a pregnant silence, accompanied by some lip biting.

"Well, we can't just walk into the camp and say, 'We're hee-yur!'" said Charcoal. Indeed, neither had given any thought to how they planned to observe humans once they had found some.

More silence.

"What we need is a disguise," said Trixie. "We need to take another shape."

"Hmmm – shape-shifting. Good idea. But you don't mean taking human form?" said Charcoal. "That makes no sense. How would we explain our sudden appearance in a camp where everyone doubtless knows everyone else?"

"No, no, of course not! We need to be more creative. How about some other creature? Hmmm … not polar bears. That's out. They'd probably start shooting at us if two polar bears suddenly strolled into camp. How about unicorns … or gryphons*?"

"I don't think modern humans believe in them anymore," said Charcoal. He recalled reading somewhere they'd been hunted nearly to extinction Down Below many centuries ago. "I'm pretty sure humans consider them legendary creatures. Haven't you noticed how the gryphons up here are always so skittish? And I know several unicorns who have nothing good to say about humans. Whales, seals, and walruses are all out, too. We're not near any open water, and it's very unlikely a whale would come strolling into camp uninvited."

Trixie added, "Or even *in*vited," and gave him a look that translated as *"Uh – duh!"* She continued, "What about a bird of some kind?"

Charcoal pondered this. "We're quite far from any bird cliffs. It would be decidedly odd for birds to fly this far out. Do you see any in the sky?" No, Trixie had to concede, there were no birds anywhere in sight. In fact, they'd not seen one the entire day, or any animal for that matter.

Suddenly she brightened. "Wait a minute," she said. "Why do we need to be creatures? Why can't we be inanimate objects? A snowdrift, say, or some pack ice, or a rocky outcrop, for instance? And it would be a much less taxing shape-shift anyway."

Charcoal agreed but said, "I don't think humans would be inclined to bring any of those things inside. I really want to have a look at them inside their habitat if possible. You know, watch them move, speak, interact, while they're unaware of us. What shape could we assume that would bring us right into the Quonsets?"

Trixie gave her cousin an appreciative glance. He knew what those bumps were called. Charcoal was full of surprises. Always.

They floated out of the ravine and cautiously glanced around the camp. The humans who had spooked Charcoal were no longer in sight. To judge from their footprints, they had re-entered the structure. A careful search confirmed no one was out and about. There, beckoning just a short distance away was a hut with a sign marked "SUPPLIES" over the entrance. Perhaps this was a good place to hide for a while, sheltered, safe, and able to develop a solid plan.

The doors were locked and the Quonset, heavily reinforced against potential bear attacks, was also thickly insulated. It wouldn't be easy getting inside *that*. But these were two highly resourceful elves (and potentially there were yummy things inside).

Ultimately, they were able to compress themselves into so fine a mist that, with some effort, they worked themselves through the air filtration system and entered the building. When they reassumed their natural shapes, Trixie just pointed and laughed (softly). "Char, you're a mess. Look how disheveled you are, and your clothes are almost as streaked as your hair!" Charcoal was sensitive to remarks about his hair, even from Trixie (who by now had become his closest – OK, *only* – friend), and he didn't appreciate her comments one bit. Besides, she was a mess as well. Her brilliant hair was several shades deeper than its usual green, and her lovely attire was totally streaked with dirt.

Turning himself momentarily into a mirror he said, "Well, have a look at yourself and see how funny you think *that* is!"

Trixie shrieked at the sight – more loudly than she intended. Within moments they heard the sound of running outside and voices saying, "What was that weird sound just now?" "I think something's in the supply hut," and the like. Desperately, they looked for a hiding place. Moments later they heard the electronic keypad beep and the front doors burst open. Charcoal had his first encounter with humans.

But the humans didn't encounter their first elves. Three humans, armed with rifles, stood at the ready, clearly expecting trouble. They looked carefully about and one of them, obviously in charge, said under his breath, "Careful, guys. Don't make a move, don't make a sound. If anything or anyone is in here, they could be dangerous."

Charcoal perked up his ears. What language were they actually speaking? After a few moments they appeared to relax. The tallest one - Дмитрий (Dmitriy) – his name tag was visible under his open coat – said, *"Vse vyglyadit khorosho. Nikakikh sledov vzloma ya ne vizhu, vse imenno tak, kak dolzhno byt'."*

Charcoal's hearts began to beat so wildly he was afraid the humans would hear them. He knew what language they were speaking. He knew the man had said "Everything looks in order. I don't see any sign of forced entry, and everything is exactly the way it should be."

It was the same language as in Dostoevsky's story. Charcoal now knew these humans spoke Russian! In his confusion outside he hadn't noted the supplies sign was written in Cyrillic* lettering. Wouldn't it be amazing if one of them was actually Dostoevsky? It was possible. Similar things happened all the time in the storybooks printed in Claustown for distribution Down Below.

There were a *thousand* questions he wanted to ask them, but he realized the extreme danger they were in, so, with great effort, he kept still and remained on high alert. He only hoped Trixie was, too. He shot a mental message to her, and she confirmed she was all right. Apprehensive, but all right.

The shortest of the trio now spoke, in a voice markedly higher than the other two. This human's name tag was also visible. It read "Екатерина" – Yekaterina. This human said, "I heard it, too. It must have been some creature outside. There's nothing amiss here. Sir, as long as we're here, might I suggest we bring in a few extra tanks of petrol for the generators?"

The one in charge nodded in agreement. The two other humans each grabbed two cans of petrol – whatever *that* was – including the one Charcoal had changed himself into. Uh-oh. This was about to get complicated. Dmitriy stopped for a moment. "This can feels light."

Immediately Charcoal increased the weight of the can. Dmitriy grunted and headed toward the main building. Charcoal didn't know how long he could keep up this shape, especially with the extra effort required to make it heavier. *We should have practiced shape-shifting for longer periods of time*, he thought regretfully.

The trio of humans, with their burden of gasoline, left the building, resetting the touchpad behind them. The one carrying Charcoal mumbled under his breath, "There's something strange about this can. I'll check it out once we get back inside. It's cold out here." Charcoal heard Trixie's voice in his head: *Char – be careful! If you need anything, just contact me. I'll be ready.*

Entering the main Quonset, Charcoal was momentarily stunned by the new sensations, sounds, and activity going on everywhere. He almost forgot to maintain his shifted shape. This was unlike anything he'd ever experienced before. He'd been in several abandoned stations, but never dreamed one in operation would be so filled with activity – and humans. For a few moments he was fascinated rather than afraid.

"Put the petrol cans over there," said the human in charge. "Sir," said Dmitriy, "one of these cans feels odd. I think we need to check it."

"Fine," said the one in charge. "Dispose of your arms and we'll have a look."

With that they all stepped farther into the structure. Charcoal looked frantically for another way out. Not seeing one, he decided to try invisibility. He'd attempted it a few times in the past – once when he was charged by an angry bull walrus –– but he knew he could only hold it for a brief while as it was very challenging.

Suddenly the odd gas can was no more. Just then Dmitriy returned. He stopped dead in his tracks, staring at the *three* gas cans on the floor. "What the …" he said aloud. "Sir!" He turned and rushed out of the room, leaving the inner door open behind him, with Charcoal, in his natural form but invisible, following right behind. Once in the next room, Charcoal looked around wildly for the best thing to transform into – something ubiquitous, unnoticeable, common.

A moment later he was a strange yellow, wooden rod with a black point on one end and a sort of pink squishy thing on the other. He joined a bunch of others in a cup-shaped holder. *I believe humans call this a pencil. I wonder what it's for?* he thought. Despite his nervousness he couldn't help but think how funny it would be if someone else was also pretending to be a pencil and hiding in the same holder. There were some yellow and a few red pencils, but no green ones … So much for that.

Dmitriy and the human in charge rushed back into the outer room and began speaking very quickly and loudly. Charcoal didn't bother to listen. He could easily surmise what was being said. He took a deep breath and tried to calm himself. *I'm getting tired,* he thought. *I don't know how much longer I can hold this shape.* Heated discussion continued from the outer room. Dmitriy did *not* sound happy. His superior even less so.

CHAPTER 15

MORE HUMANS

Just then a bell sounded. Not an actual bell, rather a spooky, artificial-sounding bell-tone. Someone cried out, "Uzhin!" and the whole room of people stood up as one and exuberantly began heading for another part of the structure, chatting and laughing just like a group of elves on one of their snack breaks. Even a very upset Dmitriy and his supervisor left and joined the others. "We'll get to the bottom of this after eating," said the one in charge, clearly perturbed. Charcoal was finally completely alone.

He resumed his natural shape with relief. Assuming a different shape was always a strain. Assuming one so substantially different in size, shape, texture, material, and color – potentially exhausting. After stretching his limbs, he wandered cautiously about the large room. It looked familiar – filled with desks, chairs, charts, books, shelves crammed with objects, but there was much equipment he didn't recognize.

Most tantalizing were the computers. There were many, seemingly everywhere, and much newer models than the ones he was used to. Charcoal had to fight the urge to sit at one and begin exploring the data stored on it. This would be a disastrous mistake, but the temptation was very strong and elves are not noted for their self-control. Still, this was Charcoal, not just your average, run-of-the-mill, bargain-bin elf, so he was able to resist – with difficulty.

Nonetheless, his photographic memory was hard at work, registering, registering. Something here might be useful to re-call in the future, and he was thoroughly enjoying the feast of Cyrillic bombarding his senses. But search as he might, he could not spot the single, all-important word: "Dostoevsky" (Достоевский). There were several "Fedors," but not one Достоевский.

Disappointed, Charcoal sighed. He was coming to realize things don't always happen as conveniently in real life as they do in storybooks. Meanwhile, the sounds of merriment – and eating (elves *love* to eat) – emerging from the mess just beyond the double doors at the end of this room beckoned. Not just the sounds, but the *smells*. The most enticing, delicious, se-ductive odors were wafting their way into Charcoal's nostrils. He'd never smelled anything like these aromas. Not a hint of gum drop, or cotton candy, or marzipan. But he did pick up overtones of mint and cinnamon. Suddenly he realized how hungry he was!

A mental message from Trixie, still holed up as a box of powdered borscht in the supply building, distracted him from his salivary glands.

Char, are you all right? Talk to me!

He telepathed back he was fine and *They're all eating. Are you hungry?*

If telepathy had upper and lower cases, then Trixie's response would have been all caps in a giant font. *YES!!!* was the immediate reply.

Well then, get on over here!

How?!

Charcoal – being Charcoal – had paid close attention when he was carried into the main building as a gasoline container. He had memorized both touchpad codes and knew how to exit the one and enter the other without having to make the extreme effort of once again misting through the air filtration system.

He shared the codes with Trixie, adding, *Be sure to lock the supply building's door behind you.*

The security cams showed the supply hut door swing open and shut and the main building's door do the same, but no one was at the monitors watching. (A week later, when the security footage was being reviewed at headquarters, all anyone saw were doors and drawers opening and closing and things moving about on their own, although the audio picked up faint voices speaking some completely indecipherable language. Apparently, security cams can't pick up elves – even when solid, luckily – unless they *wish* to be recorded. Just like cameras and cellphones. But that's a different story.)

Moments later his cousin, noticeably cleaned up, was standing before Charcoal. "What are those delicious smells?!" she exclaimed. "And how do we get at them?"

They stealthily crept through the back corridor, following their noses. The kitchen couldn't be far. Moments later, if there'd been anyone in the kitchen, they would have noticed the door from the corridor swing open, seemingly by itself. But the kitchen was empty. The chef had joined the crew at table, busy having his own dinner. Everyone in the camp was seated and enjoying their hot borscht.

"I wonder what this is …" said Charcoal as he lowered a ladle into the bubbling concoction (a ladle floating in air visible on the security cam).

"I dunno, but it sure is delicious!" responded Trixie as she practically poured it down her throat.

Elsewhere in the room roasted chicken breasts stuffed with butter and parsley, with sides of dumplings and roasted carrots, awaited their fate. They recognized these from meals at home. One thing neither recognized were green ball-shaped veggies, a tad smaller than golf balls and looking like miniature cabbages. They had an odd, bitter sort of taste – normally repugnant to an elf – but the honey glaze and bits of some sort of crispy, smoky, tangy, meat sprinkled all over them made the oddities slide down just right.

Inside the freezer they found bottles of clear liquid – "Why doesn't this water freeze?" asked Charcoal – but on tasting, the flavor was so pungently sharp and acrid, with a weird tang like rubbing alcohol, they decided against pursuing it further. In the fridge, there were stacks of a red-labeled dark liquid called "Cool Cola" looking tantalizingly like Elfdom's favorite soft drink. Upon trial, it presented a reasonable facsimile, though it was odd to be drinking them cold. You see, in Claustown beverages – pretty much everything, in fact – was routinely ingested hot.

Before long the two elves were lazily pushing their chairs back against the wall, sated and ready for a nap (not an option) after a good meal and a challenging day. That feeling evaporated when the door to the mess suddenly swung open, the chef hurrying back into the kitchen. *WOOSH!* Two empty chairs suddenly righted themselves. There was a hint of mist rising off the kitchen floor as well. Chef thought it odd but shrugged it off. He was too busy to think – he had the Chicken Kyiv to serve.

Char, telepathed Trixie mischievously. *Let's have some fun.*

What've you got in mind? he replied, intrigued.

Watch!

Out of the corner of his eye Charcoal noticed an additional platter suddenly appear on the countertop. Sparkling clean but otherwise matching the other two platters loaded with the main course. "I don't remember three of these," said the chef to himself, hastily heaping more chicken, dumplings, carrots, and brussels sprouts on the Trixie-cum-platter. Charcoal heard Trixie think, *Mmm, nice and warm!* and giggle as the chef picked her up and carried her into the mess hall.

What is *that elf up to?* thought Charcoal. He studied the room through the doorway window. Watching the humans inside and overcome with curiosity, he had his own daring idea. Choosing a nose from one crew member, eyes from another, a beard from a third, and so on, he transformed himself into a composite Arctic explorer – looking a bit like everyone else in the building. Taking a big gulp of air and squaring his new height and broad shoulders, Charcoal strode nonchalantly into the room – surrounded by laughing, eating, drinking Russians.

The crew was occupied enjoying the delicious meal. Charcoal wondered if there wasn't room for a bit more now that he had a larger stomach. Although a few gave him an odd "who's he?" sort of glance, the food was too beckoning. Charcoal figured just one more taste couldn't hurt – he wanted to blend in, after all – and he made it a point to dig the serving fork deep into the piece of chicken "on" Trixie, scraping the ends of the tongs along the platter. *Quit it. That TICKLES!* he heard. The food certainly was delicious.

All at once the room fell alarmingly quiet. The commanding officer stood up, pushed Charcoal mildly but firmly on the shoulder and said: "I asked you, who are *you?*" Everyone in the mess hall was looking at him, realizing he was unknown to them. The commander shouted, *"Answer me!"* and Charcoal, stuttering just a little, didn't quite know what to say. Suddenly he heard Trixie's voice in his head. *Disappear on the count of three. One, two, NOW!*

POOF – he was suddenly gone, right in front of everyone in the room! At that same instant a platter of food sprang off the table, everything on it flying over the crew's heads and splattering on the far wall. Pandemonium ensued.

"What happened?"

"He vanished!"

"What's going on?"

"The platter is possessed!" People were running here and

there trying to figure out what to do.

Trixie 'pathed to Charcoal: *Head for the doors, make scary noises, and push some of the crew out of your way as you run out.*

Trixie, back in her own form but now invisible, did the same. When the door to the main room flew open and slammed itself shut again, all bedlam erupted.

"We have evil spirits!"

"I'm hallucinating!"

"What did you put in that chicken?"

"This place is haunted!"

"Get me out of here."

"Captain, I resign this instant!"

Charcoal thought to Trixie, *Remind me to laugh about this later.*

As they fled out the main entrance, still howling and growling, Charcoal said out loud, "Yeti*!" The few crew members bravely in pursuit saw two enormous Abominable Snowmen suddenly striding away from camp back into the wilderness. Shocked, they just stared out the open doors, until one said, trembling and rubbing his eyes, "Yeti. *Laughing* Yeti! I can't believe what I'm seeing!" Someone stopped gaping and reached for their phone, but it was too late. The creatures were already out of sight, only footprints proving they'd actually been there. Truth be told, the gigantic Yeti-elves were laughing so hard they all but fell over as they turned the corner past a huge snowdrift. Had they been more attentive, they would have seen the snowdrift vibrating, too.

But now something else *did* catch their attention. Just around the drift stood a beautiful sight – a sparkling, candy-encrusted sleigh with two Yule Goats* hitched to it, their camping gear packed and stowed in back. One of the goats turned, looked at them and bleated, "Well done! It's time to head back to civilization. Adventure over."

They climbed in, the sleigh heading due north as the glowing sky darkened. Oddly, the large snowdrift, still shaking a bit, appeared to follow them as they moved farther away from the camp, gradually sinking into the surrounding terrain, until it vanished completely.

CHAPTER 16

REPORTING IN

The next morning Charcoal was sound asleep far past the time he usually woke. Exhausted when they returned the night before, they had agreed to wait until afternoon to reconnoiter for a post mortem* on their brief but momentous first adventure together.

Charcoal was still asleep midmorning when his computer lit up – bells ringing, whistles whistling, lights spinning and flashing. It could only mean one thing: "the Boss," as Charcoal had begun thinking of him. Charcoal dragged himself out of his bed, groggy-eyed and disheveled to the max as he clicked "answer." Santa appeared on the screen, with a look on his face unlike any Charcoal had ever seen before. "Yes, sir?" he responded, barely able to keep his eyes open.

"Is this the way you report back after a perilous mission?" asked the Top Elf. "I've been waiting all morning for you." Charcoal's eyes suddenly opened wide despite themselves. He stared blankly at the screen, not knowing what to say.

"Don't you think I deserved a report first thing this morning?"

"Isn't it first thing now?" yawned the still-tired elf.

"It's almost midday!" barked the Supreme One. It seemed he'd been sitting on pins and needles waiting to hear what happened while they were out on their own. Charcoal, still not thinking clearly, could only mumble some incoherent drivel.

"Exhausted – overslept – see straight – zonked."

Here he was, speaking one on one to the being everyone adored, and in his complete daze he had clearly done something to anger him.

Santa … anger ……. somehow these words didn't add up. Daring to look more closely at his idol, he saw a familiar twinkle in those blue eyes and a smile struggling very hard not to appear between those famous rosy cheeks.

"Sir?"

Santa guffawed, slapped his thigh (which was off-screen) and said, "Well, my lad, I certainly got you that time! Now, tell me all about it."

Charcoal just stared at the screen. "Really?" he said. "Really? Can this, uh, wait a bit … um, sir? I'm dead."

"If you were dead, we'd be having this conversation differently," responded the Great One, who clearly was enjoying himself but ready to talk and unwilling to wait another minute. Charcoal sighed, gathered his thoughts, and said, "Fine, sir, fine. Just let me pull myself together a bit. May I call you back in, say, ten minutes?"

Now it was Santa's turn to stare blankly at the screen.

Never, in the many thousands of years he had existed had anyone ever said, "I'll call you back in ten minutes." This elf was truly one of a kind. Santa chuckled and said, "Ten minutes it is. But not a moment more." He signed off.

As the fog engulfing Charcoal's brain evaporated, he couldn't believe what he had just done. And more to the point, how Santa had responded. Their relationship had changed somehow – how exactly, he couldn't say – but Charcoal distinctly had the impression some bridge had been crossed, some milestone reached, and Santa saw him in a different light. Perhaps even more importantly, he saw *himself* in a different light. He sensed things would never be the same again. Not ever.

Charcoal stumbled downstairs where his parents were patiently waiting, hands folded, at the breakfast table. A sumptuous meal had been prepared hours before – all Charcoal's favorite dishes. Chocolate soufflé, peppermint pancakes, hard-boiled maple syrup balls, rock candy tea. They beamed as he landed at the foot of the stairs, and clearly didn't mind that everything hot now had a chill on it. Charcoal appreciated their thoughtfulness but picked up the tea and headed back upstairs. "Sorry par and mar – the Boss awaits my call. Kisses."

He returned to his room, shut the door, and prepared to deliver his breakdown of the past several days to the Supreme Elf. Chuckles and Jolly simply stared at each other, dumbfounded.

"My baby!" Jolly finally managed to squeak.

"Not a baby anymore," responded Chuckles, his voice quavering.

A few minutes later Santa and Charcoal were face-to-face again and deep in discussion, Charcoal recounting how pleased he was with the way things had worked out with Trixie.

"She was a real asset," he said, "a total team member with nerves of steel. Resourceful and tougher than I would have ever imagined. I really look forward to our next adventure together."

"Excellent! Tell me everything, in detail," said Santa.

"Well, everything went pretty smoothly, especially for a debut foray …" Charcoal then proceeded to relate a very toned-down version of the past few days. By the time Charcoal was through softening it up, the polar bear attack was reinterpreted as a near-brush with a passing elderly bear, and the adventure inside the Arctic research camp portrayed more like a reconnaissance of distant humans engaged in scientific research.

Silence.

Santa looked sternly at Charcoal – as sternly as Santa *could* look, at any rate. Finally, after a seemingly interminable pause, he shifted in his chair, cleared his throat, and said, "All right Charcoal. You can stick to that story and we can cancel the entire project, or you can tell me what *really* happened."

"Um, excuse me, sir?"

"Nope," said the Head Elf. "I'll have none of this. If you

can't be painstakingly precise and honest in your debriefings, there's no point in continuing. For instance – that elderly bear decided you two were a vastly preferable alternative to fishing. She nearly killed the both of you, didn't she?"

Wide-eyed, Charcoal slowly nodded.

"And which part of turning yourselves into a gasoline can, a platter of roast chicken, and two Yeti would you consider a distant reconnaissance?"

Charcoal rolled his eyes. Yup – seeing when you're asleep and knowing when you're awake really was on the money, apparently.

Charcoal responded. "So … you *were* there, weren't you? I suspected as much."

"Ahem … My knowing when you're bad or good is pretty accurate, too," was the Bearded One's reply.

Charcoal stared at the screen, stunned. So the rumors were true – he really *did* know everything and *was* everywhere.

"Yup – pretty much sums it up." was Santa's spoken reply.

"Then you already know what happened. Was this some sort of a test? Were you baiting me? Where exactly *were* you all that time out there?"

Charcoal's audacity shocked even himself. Santa paused, looked thoughtfully at Charcoal through the cam, and after a few moments he responded, "You know, son, usually I'm not the one that gets the third degree. Generally, I'm the one who gives it."

He began to chuckle, slowly and softly at first, then a bit more loudly until he was laughing so hard tears were rolling down his cheeks.

"You're quite the something, you are, Charcoal," he said. "If ever there was an elf who could take what humans dish out and then give it right back to them, you're the one. But we're going to have to establish one hard and fast rule, m'lad. From now on, no more deceptions. Not of any kind. Our project requires total honesty and clear communication just as much as cleverness and split-second decision making. Are we agreed?"

Charcoal couldn't help from smiling. Smiling harder than perhaps he'd ever smiled before. So hard he thought his face might crack from lack of practice.

"Yes sir, sir! That's a promise I make with both my hearts, and one I shall keep. You have my word."

"Good!" responded Santa. "And what about you, Green Queen? Do I have your word as well?"

Charcoal spun around just in time to see a pile of laundry he hadn't noticed in the corner suddenly transform itself into Trixie, looking as fresh and green as ever.

"Yes, sir — you have my word as well," she said with a giggle and a curtsy.

Charcoal couldn't believe it.

"How long have you been there?" he asked.

"For a couple of hours," she replied. "I know we agreed

to wait until this afternoon to resume working, but I woke up this morning at exactly the same time I've been doing since we started training and felt just fine so I thought I'd come over in case you had as well. I must say you're quite the snorer, Cuz. And boy, were you ever knocked out!"

Charcoal couldn't believe it. They had agreed to sleep in today and if it were up to him, he'd still be asleep. Meanwhile she looked as if she'd just returned from a vacation.

"I thought you weren't ... weren't ..."

"A morning elf?" Santa completed his sentence by quoting him exactly. "Maybe she just didn't have anything compelling enough to make her one before now, hmmm?" He then looked at Trixie and said, "Do you have anything to add to today's debriefing?"

"Well, not since you straightened out my cousin, sir. Char – what *were* you thinking telling Santa all that nonsense?"

Charcoal was abashed – not an emotion he was accustomed to. But he 'fessed up.

"I didn't want Santa to cancel the project. I was worried [another unfamiliar emotion] if he knew everything that actually happened, he'd decide we weren't capable of the bigger mission."

"So you decided to lie, is that it?"

Charcoal began to object, but Santa interrupted.

"All right – not lie, stretch the truth so much it was pretty near one. But Charcoal, I admire your determination and your self-reliance. Rather than not having confidence in you, after your experiences and the way you two took care of yourselves, I have all the more. I'm willing to continue this project, as I think you both are."

The two cousins nodded their heads vehemently.

"Just bear in mind, Charcoal – you can want something *too* badly. Mistakes and disasters can happen as much from over-zealousness as from negligence. And we've already discussed honesty. All right, moving right along—"

"Excuse me, sir," interrupted Trixie, "but may I ask how *did* you know everything that happened to us? I'm not surprised, and I'm a bit relieved to know you had our backs, but where exactly *were* you? I never even suspected …"

Santa chuckled. "Let's just say I *drifted by* every so often to check on things." ("Drifted by … ah hah!" echoed the cousins together.) "And, m'lad, had you *really* been paying attention, you would've noticed there was suddenly one more red pencil in the holder, which then wasn't. And Trixie, before you get too cocky, it's a good thing you chose to hurl the platter of food at the wall before someone picked up a nice, plump dumpling, which would then suddenly have disappeared on their fork."

Charcoal and Trixie were both chuckling now.

"I especially enjoyed the ruckus you created in the mess hall. Ho, ho – a scene I won't forget in a thousand years. You two certainly had them spooked. I laughed all the way home thinking about it!"

The two cousins laughed along with him.

"Too good, too good! I haven't seen a bunch of humans so confused since we flew that experimental airship over Roswell*, New Mexico – I dunno, what? Must be about eighty years ago? And they're *still* talking about it! I can't wait to read the reports those scientists send to Moscow concerning yesterday," and he guffawed again. The two cousins were beaming.

"I have more to say," he continued, immediately changing his tone. "Seriously, I thought you both showed tremendous fortitude when faced with perilous situations. You were creative, resourceful, inventive, and brave. You make a great team, and that's very important. So – after your experiences on this trial run, I'm still in if you are."

Again, the cousins nodded their heads – so hard this time they could almost hear their brains bouncing around inside.

"Well then, onwards, upwards, and away, as I always say. Get it? Onwards? *Up*wards? Yes, well – now, downstairs with you both. There's a big, beautiful, delicious breakfast waiting for you, Charcoal, and from the looks of it I think there's plenty for a second breakfast for you, too, your Emerald Highness. Off with you now!"

Santa signed off, thinking, *Yep. That hair is certainly on the right person's head. Someday I'll need to explain to him exactly what it means … but not yet.*

The cousins bounced down the stairs. Never ever had Jolly and Chuckles seen Charcoal eat the way he ate that morning – a very *late* morning!

CHAPTER 17

REPLANNING

"Char, why do you think you were so wiped after our trial run?" asked Trixie later that afternoon when they had resumed preparing for the actual expedition. Charcoal looked at her with surprise.

"Weren't you wiped, too? That was a serious adventure we had – much tougher than anything I'd ever done before."

"True, but I mean, *why* were you so tired you slept through the entire next morning and didn't even hear me when I came in? I mean … I know I'd make a good thief, but I even stumbled over your hiking boots and you didn't budge."

Charcoal moved away from the computer and gave her his full attention. She continued.

"I was tired, too, but I slept my usual four hours and was fine when I woke up – just a little sore. You slept all night *and* well into the morning, too."

Charcoal hadn't thought of this. He had to admit Trixie might have a point. He *had* slept the equivalent of three usual nights. It stood to reason he'd be fatigued after all those exertions, but then why did she rebound easily, and he didn't?

Especially when he'd done much more wilderness explorationing than she in the past.

"I have a theory," said Trixie. Charcoal was all pointy ears.

"If you had to focus on one thing you did more on our trial run than you ever did before, what you would say it was?"

He pondered her question for a few moments. It certainly had nothing to do with excitement – he was plenty excited about the adventure, but not so much it would have fatigued him so. It couldn't be exposure to the sun, fresh air, occasional snow squalls – he'd been through many of those in the past. It even crossed his mind it might have been the stress of having another elf along for the ride, especially one as sometimes taxing as Trixie, but just as he was trying to put together a diplomatic way of saying so, it suddenly hit him.

He was a sturdy, one might even say a "strapping" young elf, in good condition and used to physical exertion. But the tremendous effort required to become invisible, compounded with shape-shifting and the unaccustomed lengths of those episodes, must have drained him.

"Do you think all the disguises I used might have worn me down?" he asked.

"Exactly!" exclaimed Trixie. "I didn't want to put the idea in your head, but we're having the same thought. You haven't done much shape-shifting before, have you?"

"No. Have *you*?" asked Charcoal, irked and a bit defensive.

"Calm down, Cuz, calm down. In fact, I have. Lots. No one knows this, but I love to go about Claustown in disguises.

I *am* a bit of a celebrity, you know." (Subtle toss of the head to permit sparkly green curls to bounce.) "I'm not saying this to brag, I just stand out. I'm naturally the type that's often the center of attention.

Charcoal rolled his eyes and sighed. "*And???*"

"And ever since the Ball, people constantly come up to me and act like they're my friends. They ask me all sorts of inane questions, ask me to pose for s-elfies with them, sign autographs. You wouldn't believe the things I've been asked to sign my name on – even someone's glass balls. I *love* to go about town and not be spotted. It's so freeing! And I almost always leave or enter my home while invisible. It keeps wagging elf tongues at bay. I mean, no one can pry into my activities if they don't even know where I am, right?"

Charcoal nodded thoughtfully.

"Anyway, I suspect that's why you were so much more fatigued than I when we returned. You dozed off in the sleigh, too, you know. You're just not used to it, and that's easily remedied. We need to build up your endurance when it comes to shape-shifting and dematerializing."

Charcoal saw this as an excellent suggestion, especially considering how much of each they'd probably be doing on a major expedition Down Below. And he told her so.

His new workout routine began the very next morning. Trixie had him do some standard ear and nose stretches, eye rolls, and full body bends – forward, sideways, backwards, and pretzel twists, followed by some light levitations, just to warm up and loosen up. Then, throughout the morning she would suddenly yell "Watch out!" or "Duck!" or "Danger!" and Charcoal would need to improvise an immediate change of shape or insta-vanish.

He found it so valuable he began returning the favor. One wonders what Chuckles and Jolly thought was going on up in his room – renamed "Base Camp" by their son – with all this shouting and dire-sounding terminology. The cousins had agreed to keep the yelling confined behind closed doors, but to gain further expertise, each afternoon, after a sugar-and-chocolate-laden lunch to keep the brain chugging, the two "adventurers-in-training" would venture into town assuming different shapes, or complete invisibility, for longer and longer stretches.

Charcoal's parents found this a bit hard to take at times, but they were also delighted. They both had come to love Trixie as if she were their own daughter. And they had never seen Charcoal so focused or positive. For the first time since the stork dropped him down their chimney. he appeared happy – *truly* happy – and, more importantly, their son appeared to be undergoing some sort of transformation. A tremendous one. Much as they fretted about what awaited the two on this exploration – Jolly in particular – they couldn't help but feel this project was having a wonderful effect on their son. "Son" … He was nearly a fully grown elf now.

"He'll be leaving us soon, Jol," said her spouse.

"Please, Chuck, one step at a time. Let's get him – get *both* of them – down there and back, and *then* we can deal with what's next."

But her hearts had already told her the same thing several times. And a similar conversation was ongoing at Trixie's home on the other side of Claustown.

The fact of the matter was, with each passing day Charcoal's self-esteem and attitude expanded before their eyes. While no one could possibly call him lighthearted or an effervescent imp, he seemed to hold his head higher, stand taller, and look about with a light in his eyes and an air of authority they'd never noticed before. Getting through each day didn't seem like an oppressive task for him any longer.

An aside:

By the way, dear readers: One thing should be noted — elves can't tell if another has assumed a shape or is invisible, even when right next to them. An elf invisible to a human is equally as invisible to another elf. Elves with more developed hearing might be able to hear invisible breathing, and those with enhanced sense of smell might detect their invisible companion's scent, but essentially, a shape was a shape and invisible was invisible.

Hence, practicing either within Claustown itself is strictly regulated. Absolutely no shape-shifting or vanishing, outside of training sessions, was permitted during regular work or school hours without special written permission — or dire emergency, of course. Strict legislation also dictated the length of time one may assume these states, that being five minutes' length, maximum, and even then, only under extremely extenuating circumstances (although holidays such as Prank Day, Disguise Day, and Post-Delivery Day are exceptions, naturally). Anyone found guilty of violating these regulations could be subjected to severe fines and public ridicule.

This might be all well and good, but how is this legislation enforced, you might wonder? It's really brilliantly simple and very effective. Elves, being elves, delight in nothing more than subjecting other elves to public ridicule and so are constantly on the lookout for transgressions. Any elf caught shape-shifting or dematerializing inappropriately could expect his colleagues to lay down the law themselves. It seems to work just fine — plus there's the consideration that most elves don't really have the need to shape-shift or vanish for any length of time regardless. Normally there wouldn't be any reason for it. So it was all pretty much a moot point.

Santa himself had formally exempted (in ornate writing on parchment stamped with a red seal and ribbons) the two cousins from this regulation, but the potential of being caught by seasoned busybodies was an excellent incentive to build their shifting or vanishing skills to expert levels. If Charcoal and Trixie could fool their fellow sharp-eyed, nosy elves, they could feel confident they'd succeed fooling pretty much anyone or anything.

Getting back to the story:

Although Trixie's disguise habit remained a secret shared only with Charcoal, he couldn't help but wonder if the Great Elf in the ice castle in the center of town didn't already know about it. *He seems to know everything,* he thought. Just then a great sea bird flew overhead and cried, "He does, he does, he does," or, at least, so it sounded to Charcoal.

CHAPTER 18

The Team Evolves

The last weeks of prep were drawing to a close. Trixie had proved her merit – more than once Charcoal wondered how successful this project would be without her, although he never quite managed to verbalize said thought within earshot. And more than once Trixie astutely perceived aspects of the assignment that her cousin had completely overlooked but then readily accepted into the plan unacknowledged. One afternoon, after an especially quiet and long session at the increasingly bedraggled-looking computer, Trixie humphed loudly, turned, looked at Charcoal with a gleam of discovery in her eye and said, with a note of triumph in her voice, "Solstice*!"

"Solstice?" replied her puzzled cousin.

"Indeed. Solstice! Or, more specifically, the Winter Solstice."

"And what about the Winter Solstice?" asked a now totally bewildered Charcoal.

"It's all about the Winter Solstice!" exclaimed his enlightened cousin.

He could almost see the glowing lightbulb floating over her head.

"I can't believe we never thought of this before. All of these customs and traditions and celebrations we've been researching all take place right around the shortest day of the year – and they seem directly related. It's the whole point of Yule."

"First there's the increasing darkness, then there's the shortest day, then celebrating as the days begin getting longer again. It's so obvious. How did we never notice this before?"

It set Charcoal to thinking. Santa had made it clear he was portrayed by many cultures as being very different in appearance from his true form – the Great Elf they had come to know and care about so fondly.

Although he hadn't mentioned it in so many words, the theme of light, the casting away of darkness, a new beginning, a promise to be fulfilled, and a reckoning of the past cycle of things, were all very clearly implied in the very nature of the season and his purpose for being.

"Trixie, you've totally put the star on the tree!" he exclaimed. "This is really important. All these different customs, all these different cultures … *This* is the commonality they all share. It's about rebirth and the return of light. You're brilliant!"

And before Trixie could start preening and feeling too puffed about herself, he mumbled, just loudly enough for her to hear if she strained, "I can see how my smarts are rubbing off on you."

She heard. And if Charcoal hadn't buried himself in his research notes just then he would have noticed her usual green aura had turned decidedly brown.

"That cousin of mine …" she grumbled, also at a volume just loud enough to be heard with effort. "I don't know why I put up with this."

But he wasn't straining and he wasn't listening. He was back to planning, adding this new bit of fantastic insight to the formula. He was sure he had used the word "indispensable," but if that were so, it somehow never made it to Trixie's ears.

One morning shortly thereafter an email appeared on their nearly exhausted computer. It could only have come from one source. There, on the screen, appeared a simple message: "It's time."

Indeed, it was. The two budding adventurers were summoned to a meeting at Santaschloss the following day. Their appointment was for eleventy in the morning. "Be prepared to be grilled and come unobserved" was the closing sentence – as if they didn't already know. Charcoal and Trixie looked at each other and nodded. They were ready.

Neither of them slept that night. They were too excited. Too much was riding on this meeting. Would it end in a green light to proceed, would Santa feel more prep time was needed, or would all their hard work these past weeks have been in vain? Sleep was impossible.

Morning dawned roseate, the sky glowing in rainbow hues of red, yellow, green, and blue, a gentle breeze kicking up. A beautiful Arctic sunrise cheered them both as the sun scraped the horizon – a bit lower now than a few weeks ago – and the ice crystals did their best to sparkle even more brilliantly. A light dusting of snow had covered the rooftops overnight. Their fatigue from lack of sleep was washed away in the beauty of this morning.

In both the Elph and Pixie households, their parents, bursting with excitement themselves, prepared super-special breakfasts in honor of the singular morning. The tables groaned with special treats including candy-coated popcorn muffins, Peeps soufflé (extra special, since they were out of season and very hard to come by this time of the year), sugar dumplings, and honeycomb waffles. The clock on the wall ticked its red and green hands and the morning flew by deliciously. Soon it was time for the duo to dress and venture forth. Their parents wished them the best of luck and sent them confidently to the Iceberg. And wept after they left.

"Unobserved" was a key word in the message from Santa. Naturally, they had a plan in mind. At 10:47 exactly, Charcoal's front door opened, his parents standing on the threshold. An elderly Faerie living across the street (and always planted strategically at the front window in order not to miss a single passerby) thought it odd that they were suddenly so passionate about their front garden. It *was* a lovely garden, but nonetheless the two of them waving, blowing kisses, wiping away tears, and blowing their noses seemed odd no matter how beautiful their arctic saxifrage looked. If one listened carefully, the sound of footsteps on the paving stones might have been heard under the general cacophony of nature worship, but no one was visible.

Two minutes later a handsome young reindeer buck, beautifully tricked out in light-blue fittings, bells jingling merrily, strutted down Kringle Boulevard. A few elves stopped for a moment to wonder whose offspring this was, as he didn't look familiar. They admired the especially proud way he carried himself and the unusual blaze of black and gray on his forehead. But there were plenty of reindeer in Claustown, so no one gave it any more thought. And when he strutted up to the Pixies' front door and Trixie's parents hitched him up to a superbly crafted green sleigh, again no one thought more of it than that the fabulous Trixie, wherever she was, was about to go for a special ride – probably to do something equally fabulous. Then, with no occupant, reindeer and sleigh took off, sliding down the street heading for the center of Claustown. Observers shrugged and continued on their way. Interesting, but not gossip-worthy.

As the equipage* pulled up at the side entrance to Santaschloss, two wooden guards looked at each other in puzzlement. They had no instructions to expect an arrival, especially one in such high style, and using a side door to boot. The fact that the sled was without passenger was even stranger. The buck snorted and pawed the pavement with his hooves. The guards came up to investigate. Things became even more confusing when the reindeer and sleigh suddenly melted into a big puddle on the street, and then vanished completely. The guards looked up, down, and every which way trying to figure out what had just happened.

Distracted, they didn't notice the small door-within-a-door in the portal crack open, then slowly shut again. "Everything seems in order," said one to the other. With that they shrugged, turned smartly, and returned to their posts – unusual happenings were part of the job description when working for Santa. But even so, this was a singular occurrence.

Had anyone been just inside they would have heard a light lilting voice, coming from nowhere, say, "It worked."

Then another, deeper voice, "Let's hold it just a while longer. Where do we go from here?"

Then a third voice, deeper and much louder, seemingly coming from everywhere, "Down the hallway, a left up the staircase, third door on the right."

* * *

Moments later two elves, dressed in their best attire, both with unusual hair, were standing before the Great One himself in his personal office. Santa looked very pleased and congratulated them on their cleverness but did mumble, "We need to look into security around here."

He turned and faced the duo. "Well?" Two expectant elvish faces, one gray-eyed and one green, looked back at him seeming as if all the world depended on this meeting. And perhaps it did.

"Well … here we are," Charcoal replied. "We're eager, we've worked like sled dogs, and we stand awaiting your word. Do we, or don't we?"

Santa, impressed by the new maturity Charcoal was showing, chuckled.

"Now, hold on. It's not so simple. I admit the two of you

think you're ready. You've certainly dedicated yourselves fully and admirably toward this project. But ..."

The glimmer of light dimmed in Trixie's eyes and she nervously played with her hair. But Charcoal boldly took a step forward, squared himself fully – reaching roughly to Santa's chest – and said, "What more do you need to know? What can we show you? What can we tell you?"

Santa cupped his chin with his hand and thought for a few moments. You could hear ice expand in the silence. "Pull up a chair, each of you."

For the next hour, Santa grilled the novice explorers about geography, history, social and political conditions, cultural differences, current world conflicts – "There's almost *always* a war going on somewhere Down Below, you know." – currency conversions, which cheek to kiss first in which country – everything he could think of that might affect, or betray, the two in their venture Down Below.

There were some questions they hadn't considered: "Who was the greatest operatic soprano of the twentieth century?" and "Why is Portugal not part of Spain?" and "What is the favorite candy of Ecuador?" But for the most part the two spoke of the human condition as if they were a natural-born part of it all. They conversed readily on the current conflict in Ukraine and the never-ending one in the Middle East. They grasped alternatives to fossil fuels better than most governments. They knew all the words to "Bohemian Rhapsody."

Finally, Santa slapped his thighs and threw up his arms.

"Wonderful! Better than I'd hoped! You two should be

commended – or perhaps committed, ho ho. There's now only one more test. I must be convinced you understand the risks, dangers, and consequences should you be found out. You understand you must be absolutely undetected. Should you be discovered, we would need to deny any involvement with your project."

Charcoal looked quizzically at the Great One and asked, "To whom would you be denying involvement? It sounds like you already have lines of communication down there."

Pause.

"Santa?"

The First Elf let out a long sigh.

"You're a smart one indeed, m'lad. Yes, it's as you suspect. Although it's always been top secret, there *has* been contact – occasional, limited, with hesitation. Part of my reluctance to let you two down there is the past track record when one of us makes contact."

"You mean Buddy, right?" asked Trixie.

Santa smiled and responded, "Yes, of course there's Buddy. His contact was recent, only a few human decades ago and, as you know, he managed to make quite a mess of it. I had to go down personally to straighten things out. Ultimately it wasn't easy erasing the memories of all those involved. But he was unauthorized. He wasn't Down Below on official business."

"Official business?" chorused the two cousins.

The Great Elf paused for a moment. "There've been others who *were* authorized."

"Others?" they chorused as an encore.

"Others," he stated emphatically. "Unfortunately, several times it did not turn out well."

CHAPTER 19

UNEXPECTED INFO

"About a hundred years ago," Santa continued, "our agent in India, under orders, began offering support and protection to a humble, soft-spoken gentleman who was developing a campaign of nonviolent disobedience. He was seeking his homeland's independence."

Santa motioned with his hands in the air in front of him. Suddenly an image of a slight, bald, dark-skinned, bespectacled man, looking harmless and unassuming, appeared before them.

"He was instrumental in establishing the modern Indian nation. A legend in the world today. And we were there to assist in any way we could." He paused a moment and his voice darkened. "He was assassinated. We didn't see it coming; missed our chance to rescue him."

He sighed, waved his arms once again and the image of a young, light-skinned girl with short-cropped dark brown hair, dressed in flashing armor, suddenly floated in the room.

"Long before that, in France, a peasant girl was summoned by voices to step forward, rebuild the nation and place the rightful king on the throne. Can you guess where those voices came from? As often happens when dealing with humans, this, too, spun out of control. She was captured, found guilty of what was termed heresy and sentenced to be burned to death." All three shuddered. "It was indeed horrible. We were able to transport her once the smoke became too thick to see she was gone, but she's not been the same since. Unfortunate, very unfortunate …"

"Even before that, a child was born in Roman Palestine. He was hailed as a savior, a hero — but people chose to misinterpret what that meant. He became a great visionary, preaching love and acceptance of all humankind, forgiveness of transgressions and peace and goodwill to all. But many wanted him to become a warrior, which was not his intention at all. We developed a support team for him."

This time Santa produced an image of a handsome sunbronzed man with long dark hair and beard and searing, intense dark eyes.

"Ironically, many call him the 'Prince of Peace.' The powers he challenged called him a blasphemer. He was condemned as an anarchist and revolutionary and, once again, tortured and murdered. There was nothing we could do to assist him. But they couldn't keep him down. His spirit was too strong. His teachings have become one of the great driving forces in human history. He's the reason one of our Delivery Days is the eve of December 25. But in true human fashion, more atrocities have been committed in the name of this gentle, loving being than any other single individual who has ever lived. What he taught has often been mangled through the centuries to suit unscrupulous humans who seek power."

"*This* is the human heritage you will find yourself up against. I could go on."

The two young elves stared at Santa in disbelief. What was in store for them if these terrible things happened despite efforts to circumvent them? Santa, hearing their thoughts, sensed he might have played too heavy a hand.

"Bear in mind, these are extreme cases. I don't want you to think you're doomed to a horrible fate. There've been many successes, too."

The cousins sighed and Trixie spoke up. "Really? We don't have a terrible destiny awaiting us Down Below?"

"No," said the Great One, chuckling to change the mood. "I just want you to understand you must be on your guard. Many other great souls have spread the message of peace and goodwill without paying a dreadful price for it."

"Thousands of years ago, in what's now called Egypt, there existed a benign, protective being. His name was Bes. One of us."

A subtle change seemed to come over Santa as he produced the image of a strange, bewhiskered, impish-looking half-human half-gnome* figure with a comical face, protruding tongue and twinkling eyes resembling in some odd way Santa himself. He stuck his own tongue out for a moment, mimicking Bes, and the resemblance was uncanny. Catching himself, he paused, wiped at an eye, chuckled, and continued.

"I have a strong affinity with him – a lighthearted protector of women, children, and the home. Champion of all good things, enemy against the forces of evil. Beloved throughout the Mediterranean world. Yes, we need more Besses in the world ...”

He paused again, smiling gently as if remembering something with wistful fondness. He snapped out of it and resumed. A wave of the hand and a supremely peaceful, radiant face with vaguely Asian features and a slight smile hovered in the air before them.

“An enlightened being in Southeastern Asia spread a philosophy of inner enlightenment and renunciation of the distractions of the material world. Revered by millions, he’s another peace-loving soul and one who didn’t meet a violent end. He received much support from us, and his modern followers still do.”

“Another, a young nobleman in medieval Italy ...” A handsome, youthful man in ragged clothing, painfully thin and with a partially shaved head, now appeared. “He renounced his family’s wealth and espoused a similar philosophy for which he remains deeply esteemed. He even became adept at speaking with animals – there’s your clue right there.”

“There are many, many others. In Meso-America*, the southwestern United States, prehistoric Turkey, the Indus Valley – to name just a few locations. Your assignment is much simpler. This isn’t a mission to spread enlightenment or reform humankind. This is a fact-finding endeavor. Just please be aware this won’t be a stroll up Sugar Plum Peak. Keep caution constantly in mind. Keep a low profile, don’t be obvious or stand out. My dears, humans can be dangerous. They can also be wonderful. Without a doubt they are *very* complicated!"

As Santa concluded, the two young elves sat silently, staring out the castle windows. They hadn't anticipated anything like this. Charcoal stirred.

"Well, that was humbling, and more than a little disturbing."

Santa smiled. He'd clearly made the impression he'd wanted. He patted Charcoal's shoulder.

"All those projects involved direct interaction with the human species. There was success as well as epic failure. Humans seem determined to continue behaving self-destructively, sometimes as individuals, sometimes en masse. And looking about, it appears to be getting even worse. Honestly, I hadn't planned on giving true peace-on-earth-goodwill-toward-men another try at this point in time, but, well, Charcoal, you must admit you brought the project to me. I didn't approach you."

"Yes, Santa, true."

"And you want this to be a reconnaissance fact-finding mission, not direct and open contact."

"True again."

"I underscore as firmly as possible you must *not* reveal your true selves in any way, shape, or form to humans. Too dangerous. And no one must suspect you have anything humans would consider magic powers or special super-human abilities. If that were to happen … Let's just say I don't want to risk losing two elves who have not only proven themselves well above the cut, but of whom I've truly grown very fond."

With that, Trixie spontaneously leapt from her chair and gave Santa a tremendous, very long hug. Santa returned it willingly. Charcoal watched nervously, uncomfortable with this heartwarming display of affection — and also a bit envious that this was so easy for her.

"Ah, it's been a long time since I've been hugged like that — not since my Macy's* days. Mmmm. Felt good — but that's exactly what must be avoided when you're Down Below. We can't have any emotional interaction between you and humans — too dangerous. But mental note to self: More hug breaks. Especially as we approach Delivery Days."

Charcoal, having endured their tender exchange as long as he could, dissolved the warm and fuzzy mood with a question.

"Sir," he interjected, "if I may ask ... It sounds as if you personally have been in contact with certain key players in the human world from time to time. Am I correct?"

"Correct! And — no. You see, m'lad, there *has* been actual Santa-to-human contact in the past, but only during moments of deepest, direst need. If you look back at history, there have been moments — true turning points in human history — where it seemed some sort of what humans would call intervention suddenly straightened out a situation verging on disaster. Apollo XIII* for instance. Or the collapse of the Iron Curtain*. Or Attila* not sacking Rome."

Because of their intensive studies, the cousins were aware of all of these examples.

"All you?" asked Charcoal.

"I don't mean to brag, but all me," replied the Number-One Elf.

"There've been misses, too. Still regret not making it to Ford's Theatre* in time. And if I'd spotted what was pending in Sarajevo* back in 1914 …"

Santa fell silent for a long moment.

"The point is, apart from Delivery Days, my interaction with Down Below is never intentionally blatant. *Subtle intervention*, that's the ideal. The few times it was necessary for me to actively involve myself, we arranged that immediately afterward it would all be wiped from human awareness. Believe me, memory deletion is not easy, especially when it involves many brains."

"Anonymity is essential. You now grasp how volatile humans can be. Even those who truly mean well can accidentally create dangerous situations. Keep them in the dark, I say. This is how we've protected Up Top all these centuries. What they can't see, doesn't exist – even if they secretly want it to. If Claustown were visible from Down Below, especially nowadays with satellites and spy-planes, well … one last time: It's *crucial* you don't reveal yourselves."

"Sir," chimed in our hero once again. "If you, or we collectively, have the ability to eliminate recall the way you describe, couldn't we somehow reprogram human brains to be less aggressive? Couldn't we mandate peace-on-earth-good-will-toward-men on a cerebral level?"

Santa fell silent yet again. *This lad doesn't miss a thing,* he thought. *That hair ...*

"On paper your suggestion makes total sense and I suppose, yes, theoretically something like that would be possible. But bear in mind we're dealing with almost eight billion human beings. The logistics are staggering and completely beyond the abilities of our tiny community, even if every single elf in Claustown were to combine forces – and how likely is that? Plus, there's an ethical aspect to your question that can't be ignored. Is it morally right to brainwash humans into behaving as we want them to, even if the good of the entire planet were at stake? This is a loaded subject indeed, my friend. But leave it to you to ask it."

He chuckled again and patted Charcoal's head. Charcoal forced himself to not pull away.

The cousins' brains were spinning. They were approaching overload ...

"Oh! One more thing," said Santa. "Something to always be aware of as you travel the globe."

"More?!" the cousins echoed despondently.

Santa looked to his right, his left, then leaned forward and lowered his voice to a whisper for emphasis.

"You need to know about the Hamn*. If they learn of your project, there's bound to be trouble."

"The Ham?" asked Charcoal, puzzled.

"HamN – the Hamn, with an N at the end. Never heard

of them, have you? Well, that's exactly the way they want it. The Hamn might prove to be your biggest challenge – but again, only if they're aware you're on a mission Down Below. Take note, my friends."

CHAPTER 20

UNWELCOME INFO

Santa continued. "The Hamn are illusive creatures originally hailing from the Antarctic*. They're the direct opposite of us, and I don't mean just geographically. They spread chaos and maliciousness all about the world. The indigenous people of Tierra del Fuego, the Selk'nam, knew of the Hamn, but because they could only hear and not see them, believed they were ghosts. They didn't grasp they were living creatures intent on doing them harm. Today, very few of that tribe survive, and modern humans know nothing about the Hamn. That's exactly what they want. It allows them to carry out their plans without humans realizing what they're up to. I suspect they're a kind of troll, actually."

The cousins' eyes grew wider. "Aren't trolls malevolent?" whispered Trixie.

"Well, yes, generally. That's why you must be so wary of them," replied the Great One. "The Hamn *hate* Yule. Abhor it – everything it stands for. Would do anything to interfere with peace-on-earth-goodwill-toward-men and have tried many times in the past to disrupt operations. The bad toy-factory fire in Claustown a hundred years ago? Hamn sabotage!

Floods? Avalanches? Landslides? You guessed it. The Bermuda Triangle*, pandemics, armed conflict, crop circles, nuclear reactor meltdowns, the internal combustion engine ... All can be traced back to the Hamn."

"I've often wondered if the lack of belief in me these days is their doing. It wouldn't surprise me if they've learned how to enter human minds. They're secretive, cunning, conniving – brrrrrr, a bad lot all around. Be on the lookout at all times and hope they don't get word of your mission. I can't guarantee there aren't spies afoot, even right here in Claustown."

Trixie and Charcoal sat quietly for a moment and let this lovely surprise sink in.

"Well, sir, what do they look like? What should we be on the lookout for?" asked Charcoal.

"That's just it," replied Santa. "No one really knows. They're said to have a ghastly white pallor about them – very handy as camouflage down by the South Pole. Some describe them as whale-like creatures with human legs and no tail. I can't picture it. Others say they're covered in a fine coat of silky thick white fur. Some say they have glaring red eyes and fangs. As I mentioned, many say they have no bodies at all – that they're actually ghosts. It seems humans can't see them, but I'm confident some other creatures can. This would explain the influence they seem to have on the species and their ability to get around the globe unnoticed."

"You can definitely hear them. They shuffle when they walk – that's the reason I always keep the area around Claustown lightly dusted with fresh snow. You can spot their tracks when they've been lurking and hear them when they try to sneak up behind you. The patrols are always on watch for them."

"They also have a distinctive scent. They like rotten fish. Devour them, actually. They'll haul a whole net of fish up onto the shore and leave them in the sun for hours to get them just the way they like 'em. And so, they reek of spoiled fish … Nasty business! You'll definitely want to avoid any Hamn whose path you chance to cross."

Trixie was very quiet – unusual for her. She stared at the ceiling apprehensively and then asked, "Are they … are they shape-shifters?"

"A very good question. I wish I had a very good answer, but I don't. I suspect they *are* shifters. We have very little solid info – they're so secretive they make us look like we're a marching band at the Tournament of Roses Parade*."

The two youngsters didn't know exactly what this meant, but they sensed his meaning.

"We do know, without doubt, of their distinct scent and their pallor. I'd say if you encounter someone deathly pale reeking of rotten fish, get as far away as you can as quickly as possible."

With that thought Santa stood and shook himself from bottom to top as if he were wiping the whole topic off his Bermuda shorts. The three of them fell atypically silent thinking about invisible deathly white evil Hamn and rotten fish.

It occurred to Charcoal what was being discussed was the "doing" and not the "maybe-ing." He roused himself and seized the moment.

"So, sir, stinky trolls and dangerous humans aside, what more do we need to discuss?"

Trixie nodded vigorously. They both made it very certain they remained committed to the project. Santa had dug himself into a hole – but a hole he didn't want to climb out of.

"Well then, if you insist. I've done my best to prepare you in every way I can think of. Let's hear what you've planned," he responded, relaxing in his easy chair and looking comfortable for the first time in a while.

"Well, sir… first stop is Russia," stated Charcoal emphatically. Trixie pointedly stared at him.

"Really?" asked Santa. "Russia is a very large country, you know. And right now, a country at war. What is it you expect to find there?"

Charcoal perked up considerably. He blurted, "Sir, since I've read *Crime and Punishment*, or most of it, anyway — which gave me the idea for this whole project in the first place — and it's a Russian novel, it seems a good place to begin. From what I've learned, there's a tradition of pessimism there I'd like to examine. I find it so — so — *compelling*."

"Anyone in particular you're planning to meet while in Russia?" responded Santa with a certain emphasis to his voice.

"No, no, sir, not really" — Charcoal crossed his fingers — "just explore and observe. I understand Yule traditions there are no longer prevalent. I'd like to see how this lack affects the inhabitants. Besides, it's relatively close to us and we've already encountered Russians briefly."

Santa looked at him in that almost annoying way he had of seeming to know more than you wanted him to.

Charcoal continued quickly. "And then — well, the world is large, with many different cultures. I think we need to examine a lot of different belief systems — both believers and non. We don't have much time, so we need to cover a lot of territory and not linger anywhere."

Santa could find nothing amiss with this logic and sat there nodding, but this was all news to Trixie, who continued to stare at her cousin. During all their preparation they'd never actually discussed a specific itinerary. She had daydreamed about beach time on the French Riviera and hiking in the Andes.

Russia? she thought.

CHAPTER 21

IT BEGINS

"So, what's this about Russia?" Trixie, in a huff, asked on their way home. She didn't feel the need for a disguise once they'd left the center of town, but Charcoal wanted to practice more, so he shape-shifted as a gryphon upon whose back she rode. She was oblivious to the awed glances, the jabber, and the finger-pointing of the elves they passed. In her annoyance, she didn't even bother to telepath. "When, pray tell, was Russia decided upon, please?"

"Well, it *was* how this whole project started, you'll recall," responded Charcoal-cum-gryphon defensively. "And there's someone there I really need to meet."

Trixie knew exactly who that someone was. She could only hope this wouldn't become a great big time suck. Santa had agreed to two weeks Down Below. "Not a nanosecond longer" were his exact words. Two weeks! On the one hand, it seemed like an eternity — two weeks among humans. How dreadful. On the other, like the blink of an eye. What could possibly be accomplished in just two weeks? Would there be time for the Cote d'Azur*? And she longed to visit those spectacular mountains in Zhangjiajie*, too. Trixie switched to telepathy.

So you've already mapped out part of our itinerary without including me in the decision-making. Starting in Russia is fine. I have no problem with that, but I wish you had included me in your thinking rather than surprising me with a done deal. And to boot, you've started with a half-truth to Santa! Pray tell, what am I supposed to be doing while you meet this Dusty Elfsky guy?

Dostoevsky. You're welcome to come along, only you can't talk much. I have so many questions and there's so little time. But I must find an hour or two.

An hour AT MOST! she responded crossly.

Sometimes that cousin of hers … Anyone looking very closely would've spotted a small green cloud over the Green Queen's head. The gryphon she rode looked a trifle abashed.

* * *

The next few days were spent in intensive final preparations. Last-minute things needed doing. Apart from his parents, no one would particularly miss Charcoal, but Trixie's scarcity had already been noted and frequently commented upon. She would need a plausible excuse for an extended absence. A sick uncle? No. If she had one, everyone would already know. A beauty pageant? No. Where would an elf from Claustown go to compete? A retreat? Hmmm … a retreat. Unusual, but not far-fetched. She could claim Santa had offered her his country house, Tinseltonia*, as a getaway where she could practice singing, dancing, and baton twirling for the upcoming gala launch of this year's Production Season*. She could arrange with Santa to spend an overnight there so it wouldn't actually be a lie. Neither Trixie nor Charcoal were comfortable lying but, as we just saw, bending the truth (an elf specialty) was another thing. They both knew there'd be plenty of truth-bending in store for them in the coming two weeks, like it or not. Might as well start practicing now. In the meantime, they threw themselves fully into their remaining prep time.

The night before they left, Santa invited the two families – totally undercover, of course – to a lovely dinner at the Iceberg both to acknowledge the pending endeavor and to make absolutely certain their parents were completely on board with the expedition. Naturally, there were anxieties, but Santa took the elder Elphs and Pixies aside (they were in total awe of their surroundings and host) and assured them he would arrange for "certain associates" to keep track of their offsprings' activities and intervene if ever needed. He truly believed, even with the obvious risks, the pair would fare well and return safely. He also felt it best the two adventurers were unaware they would be protected — protected as much as possible at any rate. "Character-building," he called it. What he really meant was insurance — they wouldn't be careless thinking he'd be there to intercede if something went wrong. Production Season was soon to start up, and his attention would be divided at best.

While the folks feasted on a dessert of marzipan/lychee/sugar-lump ice cream, he met separately with the duo for some last instructions.

"You know very well there are risks involved in this adventure – risks I feel you grasp and believe you can deal with. However ... in case any situation truly gets out of hand, you can send out an SOS of sorts. The distance will be too great to converse telepathically from here, but there are others Down Below who'll try to assist, if and when they can.

"Others?" queried the two stuffed and excited young elves.

"Yes. You'll rarely be so far away from an agent you can't summon help – mind you, strictly in dire circumstances. Their hands are already full with their own assignments, so don't be bothering them unless there is true peril."

The two nodded vigorously. Santa was about to set them loose when Charcoal cleared his throat.

"Um – and, strictly in true peril, how would we call for help?"

Santa chuckled. "It would be just like me to send you off without a secret code word, wouldn't it?" Neither thought this likely but they pretended to agree. "Hmmm … now, what shall it be?"

Santa thought for a moment and then looked up again. "The secret code is '*eoteltsim*' – 'mistletoe' backwards. Say it three times in succession – only in extreme need, mind you – and help will be there – *if* available."

"Eoteltsim?" asked Charcoal.

"Eoteltsim," said Trixie.

"Eotelt—"

"Shhh!" interrupted the Great One. "Only in extreme need. Let's not call anyone away from their own projects when there's no need to. Save it for a true emergency – which is unlikely if you're smart and cautious. And let's keep this info strictly among ourselves. No one else" — he cocked his head toward their parents in the next room — "need know."

"But there are *no guarantees*. Absolutely keep that in mind. An agent might be unavailable, or you might be out of range. Ultimately, it's up to *you* to anticipate potential trouble and keep out of harm's way."

The idea of a secret codeword tickled Charcoal no end, and made Trixie feel even more special than usual, but it also had the double-edged effect of underscoring they were leaving a place of safety and familiarity for a very different environment. No telling *what* might befall them over the next two weeks. The codeword was a very reassuring safety valve — in case of *extreme need*. And *no guarantees*.

As they headed to their respective homes after an unforgettable evening, both delightful and mildly disquieting, a thick mist began to engulf Claustown, obscuring them from prying eyes. Santa's doing? The duo thought they knew the answer. A blanket of fog would cover their departure all the better. Definitely a bonus.

After careful consideration, it had been agreed they were to leave the next morning just prior to sunrise. By dawn, late-night revelers would have returned from their carousing and be snug in their beds, while early-bird workers were yet to rise. It was the perfect time for two dim figures, hidden in the thickest pea-souper anyone in Claustown could recall, to slip past the guards at the main gate with no need for energy-taxing invisibility.

And so, just moments after the sun would've been seen changing direction on a clear day, two silhouettes, stirring the fog around them, did just that. But this time, no watchful snow drift followed them. Their adventure had begun. This time they were on their own.

To Be Continued...

GLOSSARY

BOOK ONE: UP TOP

Antarctic – the region located at the southernmost part of Earth.

Apollo XIII – the seventh crewed mission in the Apollo lunar project, the third intended for lunar landing. Fifty-six hours after its launch in 1970, an explosion onboard made it impossible to complete its mission. Against the odds, the crew managed to return to Earth safely.

Arctic – the region located at the northernmost part of Earth.

Attila – king of the Huns from 434 to 453 HR (Human Reckoning). One of the greatest of the "barbarian" kings who invaded the Roman Empire, he terrorized the Balkans, Greece, Gaul, and Italy. Legend says he was persuaded not to sack Rome itself, turning away at its very gates.

aurora borealis – a natural display of colorful lights of various shapes appearing in high-altitude skies, mostly during winter months, caused by solar winds affecting the magnetosphere. (See *northern lights.*)

biped – a creature that walks on two legs.

Bermuda Triangle – an area of the North Atlantic Ocean

loosely defined by Bermuda to the north, Miami to the west, and Puerto Rico to the south, in which mysterious occurrences including ship and airplane disappearances are said to have happened.

Busy Season – the time of the year *Up Top*, commencing after high summer, when production kicks up in anticipation of *Delivery Days*.

Claustown – the town in which *Santa*, his family, and community of elves reside. Located at *the North Pole*.

Claustown Civic Center – the municipal building for *Claustown*, housing the town offices and used for political and community events in its Grand Assembly Hall.

Cote d'Azur – aka the French Riviera, fronting the Mediterranean Sea in Southern France.

Cottingley – a town in West Yorkshire, England, where photographs taken in 1917 of two young girls interacting with *fairies* created an international sensation.

Crime and Punishment – a book by Russian author *Fyodor (Fedor) Dostoevsky*, first published in 1866.

Cyrillic – a writing system for various languages spanning Eastern Europe and Asia.

Delivery Days – the annual dates when *Santa*, in various guises, makes his rounds. Dates range from December 6 to January 6.

Delivery Season – the time of year following late autumn when all *Claustown* prepares for *Delivery Days*.

diatonic scale – a music scale consisting of seven notes per octave.

Dostoevsky, Fyodor (Fedor) – renowned Russian author (1821–1881), considered one of the greatest novelists of all (human) world literature.

Down Below – the popular phrase for all lands situated below the North Pole elf domain.

ennui – from the French; a feeling of boredom or "seen it all before." Listlessness. Dissatisfaction.

Elf Elders of Yore / Elfstory – the authors and recorded history of *Elfdom*.

Elfdom – the inclusive community of elves residing at the *North Pole*; includes *Claustown* proper and its outskirts. Elves residing elsewhere on the planet (*Down Below*) are not Elfdom, but considered related.

Elfish – the universal language of elves, with regional variants. Can also mean possessing elf-like qualities (in that sense, **elfish**).

Elfstory Annals – the group of sagas of the history of *Elfdom*. Transmitted orally for generations, they have now been compiled into a series of twelve volumes housed in the *Saint Nicholas Memorial Free Library* in *Claustown*, available for research by special request.

Elph – one of the four elf clans residing in *Claustown*. They claim to be the original, and therefore, oldest of the four clans.

equipage – a carriage, horses, and all associated equipment used for equine transportation.

Faerie – (in this sense) one of the four elf clans residing in *Claustown*. Different from "fairy" as the common spelling.

faren - "enough" in common *Elfish*.

Ford's Theatre – the location in Washington, DC, where American president Abraham Lincoln was assassinated in 1865.

gnome – a small, humanoid creature. Believed by humans to be mythological.

Great Elf Code – the impressive compilation of laws, regulations, and suggestions governing all *Elfdom*, assembled in the year 1823 HR (Human Reckoning) and engraved in the solid ice over the dais in the Council Room of *Wenceslaus Hall*.

Great Selection Ball – the gala event held in *Wenceslaus Hall* upon the graduation of second-year elves where their assignments in various workshops are announced. One of the greatest highlights of the elf year.

gryphon – a creature with a lion-like body, an eagle-like head and wings, and talons for front feet. Believed by humans to be mythological.

Iron Curtain – the imaginary dividing line separating Europe into contrasting political entities in the mid-twentieth century.

Hamn, the – illusive, intensely malevolent creatures from the Antarctic, known and feared by the Selk'nam, an indigenous people of Tierra del Fuego but entirely unknown to modern humans. Possibly related to *trolls*, they are tall, often over two meters (six feet, seven inches) in height, strong, covered in fine white fur, their heads having the appearance of being located in their chests. Their piercing red eyes can be hypnotic. They shuffle rather than walk and are said to reek of the rotten fish they eat in large quantities. They are dedicated to the overthrow of *Yule* in all its forms and attributes.

Iceberg, the – (in this sense) *Santa*'s ice castle. (See *Santaschloss.*)

icosikaipentatonic scale – a music scale consisting of twenty-five notes per octave.

Jack Frost – famed Claustown abstract artist, esteemed even Down Below for his ice paintings, which only survive at temperatures below the freezing of water.

Macy's – world-famous department store founded in New York City in 1858 HR (Human Reckoning) and host of the annual Thanksgiving Day Parade ending with an appearance by Santa Claus.

marzipan – a sweet paste of ground almonds, sugar, and egg whites.

matryoshka – Russian nesting dolls.

Meso-America / Mesoamerica – a region beginning in the southern part of North America, extending to the Pacific coast of Central America, including the human countries of central and southern Mexico, Belize, Guatemala, El Salvador, and parts of Honduras, Nicaragua, and Costa Rica, containing remains of several highly developed early native civilizations.

Midnight Sun – popular term for when the sun remains visible above the horizon at midnight at high altitudes during certain times of the year.

narwhal – a species of toothed whale, having a spiral, horn-like tooth, projecting unicorn-like from its snout, frequently found in Arctic waters.

Non-Aggression Clause – legislation preventing members of different elf clans from physical or verbal aggression during mutual litigation and negotiation.

Non-Delivery Season – the time of the year when gift production in *Claustown* is at a more relaxed pace. (See *Delivery Season*.)

North Pole – in this context also called *the Pole*. The northernmost end of the axis of rotation on Earth. Also, an alternate name for *Claustown*.

northern lights – see *aurora borealis*.

pentatonic scale – a music scale consisting of five notes per octave.

Pixie – (in this sense) one of the four elf clans residing in *Claustown*.

post mortem – Latin for *after death*. In this sense, meaning review and analysis of an event or project after completion.

précis – a summary.

Production Season – the period in a typical elf year when heightened production of gift items is underway prior to *Delivery Days*. Generally, there is a month's lull between the fulfillment of the final *Delivery Day* of any annual cycle and the gradual resumption of production at a reduced pace.

Quonset – a structure of corrugated metal, shaped like a half-cylinder, easily constructed and very durable.

Registration Day – the annual day when newborn elves are officially introduced to the community and registered by name, date of birth, and parentage in the official *Claustown* archives. The event includes a formal procession.

Roswell – a city in southeastern New Mexico (USA) notorious as the purported location of a 1947 "UFO" crash.

Saint Nicholas Memorial Free Library – the magnificent public library in *Claustown*, donated many hundreds of years ago by *Santa Claus*. Subjected to frequent closings due to lack of interest.

SANTA / SANTA CLAUS (aka **Saint Nick, Kris Kringle,** etc.) – the iconic, adored elf in the red suit, ruler of *Claustown*, symbol of *Yuletide* and bringer of the joy the season connotes. Delivers gifts around the world from December 6–January 6, although often in alternate forms (see below).

(Elf nicknames for Santa include the Bearded One, the Elf of All Elves, the First Elf, the Great Elf, the Great One, the Head Elf, the Number-One Elf, the Supreme Elf, the Supreme One, and the Top Elf.)

Some of Santa's alter-egos mentioned in Book One:

old kindly witch – Befana, mostly an Italian tradition but a similar tale is common in Eastern Europe (**Babushka**).

a scary horned creature – Krampus, a frightening central European creature, half-goat, half-demon, who punishes wicked children but also assists with distributing gifts to those warranting them.

a queen – Mab, Queen of the Fairies, mostly in the British Isles and Canada, who has delivered gifts in human stockings for over 800 years.

Christkind – a beautiful queen or fairy who brings gifts to children throughout Germanic cultures.

a dwarf – Nissemenn are dwarves of Nordic tradition who deliver gifts and make mischief, also reported from Kentucky through rural New York State (USA). It is rumored these are actually carefully selected elves assisting *Santa* with delivery.

Three Kings – a tradition in many lands on various dates, mostly January 6. *NOTE: Santa often mentions splitting into multiple beings (kings, dwarves, etc.) allowing him to make his rounds more quickly.*

s-elfie – a photographic image of an elf taken by itself using a photographic device such as a camera or human cell phone. The image will only register if the subject is willing to be photographed. An elf cannot be photographed when they have shape-shifted. *Note: Since elves can communicate telepathically, telephones of any kind are not used* Up Top.

Santaschloss (aka "the Iceberg") – Santa's palatial residence in *Claustown.* Constructed mostly of ancient, excavated ice, the edifice contains numerous public and private council chambers, a throne room, formal reception rooms, and the dwelling chambers of *Santa Claus,* his family, and retainers, when in residence.

Sarajevo – capital of Bosnia and Herzegovina and location of the 1914 assassination of Austrian archduke Franz Ferdinand, which triggered World War I.

simpatico – Italian for having shared interests, compatibility.

slaxi – a reindeer-drawn sleigh and driver for short-term hire.

solstice – when the sun reaches its northernmost or southernmost points marked by the longest or shortest day.

South Pole – the southernmost end of the axis of rotation of the Earth.

Spright – (in this sense) one of the four Elf Clans residing in *Claustown*.

Sugar Plum Peak (aka "the Peak") – the most prominent geographical feature of *Claustown*, towering above the community. Open to the public although unfrequented, much of it is landscaped with hiking paths.

telepathy – mental communication from one being to another. "Telepathing" or "'pathing" (v.) describes communication in this method.

Tinseltonia – Santa's country retreat, in the wilderness south of *Claustown*.

toadstool – a mushroom poisonous to humans.

Tournament of Roses Parade – annual parade in Pasadena, California (USA), on January 1 known for elaborate, flower-covered floats.

troika – a Russian sled pulled by three horses abreast.

trolls – mischievous or malevolent creatures dedicated to creating chaos. They may be extremely large or tiny. Humans believe them to be mythological.

unicorn – a rare woodland creature with a single horn projecting from its forehead. In Europe, they resemble horses. Believed by humans to be mythological.

Up Top - the popular term for the *North Pole* and adjacent elf territories.

Uzhin – the Russian word for "dinner."

walrus fever – a malady unknown to humans but potentially fatal to elves. It is contracted through contact with infected walruses.

Wenceslaus Hall – The landmark Claustown ceremonial center, named in honor of kindly King Wenceslaus of Bohemia (an elf), where formal events are held throughout the year.

Yeti – a large creature similar to a bear or human covered in black, brown, or white hair, inhabiting the Himalayas. Many humans believe them to be legendary.

Yule / Yuletide – an extremely ancient human festival celebrating the change of seasons marked by the shortest day of the year and originally involving nature-based rituals. In modern times it has become heavily commercialized.

Yule Goat – a goat-like creature, frequently invisible, that supervises holiday preparations and delivers gifts, often in collaboration with Santa.

Yuletide Square – The main square of *Claustown*, located directly in front of *Santaschloss*. An enormous evergreen *Yule* tree is erected there annually.

Zhangjiajie Mountains (Hunan Zhangjiajie National Forest Park) – in Zhangjiajie, Hunan Province, China's first national forest park (1982 HR) with an area of 11,900 acres. The most notable geographic features are the towering pillar-like formations seen throughout the park, a distinct hallmark of the landscape, frequently found in many ancient Chinese landscape paintings.

ACKNOWLEDGEMENTS

To my focus group, who urged me repeatedly and with no doubt in their minds to proceed with this project: Roberta Belulovich, who read the entire book out loud with me just to make sure it scanned properly, re-proofed the final manuscript with a fine-toothed comb and never ceased to encourage me; Gabriella Belli, who loved it so much she couldn't wait to pre-order copies as gifts to her list; Alice Chebba Walsh, for her intense encouragement and insight; Elena Belli, who read it carefully with a critical eye; Laura DeMarco, whose enthusiasm and support kept the project moving forward; Peter Rezkalla for his deeply valuable critique of the Introduction; Antonella Severo, who nitpicked me in the best possible way; Dayle Vander Sande for his tireless support and input; and Carol Chebba King for being my Glaring Error Spotter.

To Michele Manduchi and Marissa Braddock, who listened to the first five chapters the day after I wrote them, encouraged me to continue, and added, "It needs dialogue."

To retired editor and walking companion Nancy Macagno, who read a draft, bought me a round of drinks, looked deeply into my eyes and said, "I think you've really got something here. Have you considered making it a trilogy?"

To Carole Teller, whose ear and heart were always there for

me, talking me off the ledge countless times and Robin McKenna who talked me down when Carole wasn't available.

To Carl Raymond and Lynn Mandel, who shared profound knowledge of the publishing industry and were essential in my decision-making in so many ways. And to Tom Miller ("A Daytonian in Manhattan") for his own insightful copy edit input.

To my brilliant and dedicated copy editor Patty Economos (foolproofcopyedit.com) for patiently wading through my extremely creative syntax and punctuation, and to Elizabeth Randolph for recommending her to me.

To my intrepid publicist, Shay Pantano, who is determined to make Charcoal a household name.

To my indomitable, persistent, and determined cover artist, John Bates (@bater_designs), who found Charcoal's face and drew it for the world to see.

And, finally, to Charcoal himself, for breaking into my home and persuading me to set his story down in words.

ABOUT THE AUTHOR - Brooklyn-born R. A. Bellson is a seasoned storyteller, award-winning videographer, avid historic preservationist, and NYC history buff. He is also a professional singer and pianist with performance credits in North America and Europe, having resided for extended periods of time in Italy, Spain, France, and Sweden.

photo: Monica Hollender

An advocate for mutual respect and tolerance, R.A. Bellson is dedicated to making a better society in which to live – possibly explaining why Charcoal D. Elph chose him to tell his tale.

Bellson holds degrees in Architecture and Museum Education and Administration, and has extensive experience writing speeches and presentations, scripts, and media releases. He maintains a home in Ocean County, New Jersey.

Charcoal the Elf, Book One: Up Top, the first in a three-part series of books, is R. A. Bellson's first work as a novelist.

...Coming Soon...

CHARCOAL THE ELF
Book Two: Down Below
Book Three: Hunted